THE SACRED SPRING
OF THE
BLOOD ROYAL

THE SECRET ORDER OF THE GRAIL

MARK STANLEY

Ascension Press

The Sacred Spring of the Blood Royal
The Secret Order of the Grail
Mark Stanley
Copyright © 2013 Ascension Press
Printed in the United States of America

ISBN-13: 978-1481957106
ISBN-10: 1481957104

In this work of fiction, the characters, places and events are either the product of the authors imagination or they are used entirely fictitiously. The publisher does not have any control over, and does not assume any responsibility for author or third-party websites or their contents.

Cover design by Alexandra Shostak
coversbyalexandra@gmail.com

CONTENTS

This is a work of fiction.
And yet:

The Prieuré de Sion is a secret order that has
its roots in the ancient mystery schools, but
was formally created in 1099 A.D. during the
inception of the First Crusade.
For centuries members of the Prieuré de Sion
have been the targets of assassinations.
Only recently, several members died in one
year of "brain hemorrhages".

1

The Innocent

I was born in the winter on a cold, crisp, starry night. My earliest memories are of the distant sounds of waves relentlessly crashing on a stony beach, and the melange of aromas of the creatures of a saltwater inland Sound: cod, oyster, clam, geoduck, seaweed, octopus and salmon. I came into this world in the year 1923 in the Pacific Northwest. It is a land of rain, sun, water and snow.

I was raised by my mother and given the name Marc Remillard. I never knew my father. He died at sea shortly before I was born.

We lived south of Seattle in a sleepy neighborhood of beach houses above Three Tree Point. The prominence juts out into Puget Sound, with the sea floor rapidly dropping to the depths of 500 feet below sea level. The only claim to fame Three Tree Point has ever had is that the largest octopus in the world was caught a hundred yards off of the shore there.

It was the kind of neighborhood where people

generally didn't lock their doors. There was simply no need for such precautions. It was a rural enclave that went unnoticed by the rest of the world. Except for the little store nearby, the closest business establishment was a mile away over a difficult, contorted road.

I was a child of the Great Depression that began in 1929. The Puget Sound region was not affected by the economic collapse as dramatically as some other areas due to the thriving timber and fishing industries, and the small farms in the valleys with their deep, fertile, glacial soils that had sloughed off of Mt. Rainier sometime in the geologic past. The Pacific Northwest is one of those rare areas that could function quite well on its own even if it were isolated from the rest of the world.

For whatever reason, I began my sojourn here imbued with a gift—a simple thing really.

Occasionally I will look at a person or people and know things about them that in no normal way should I be able to know. The depth of the perception is at times uncanny, with the hallmark being that what I perceive is always the truth. It has to be, since it has nothing to do with intelligence, conjecture or calculation. It is simply a plain clear knowing. I just *see* it.

For that reason, at a young age I began calling those moments of perception "*truth pictures*". They are indeed akin to photographs except that the lenses are my eyes and the film is processed instantaneously inside of my head somewhere.

Lets say that I am in the passenger seat of a car, and we stop to wait for a pedestrian to cross the street. When I look at him, I realize that *he is deeply frustrated because his brother has recently died, but he doesn't have enough money for the train fare to attend the memorial service on the other side of the country.* That's all I see—just a snapshot.

I have no control of when it will occur.

It took some time before I realized that others did not possess the same ability. I spoke to my mother about it once, and was surprised by her response. She studied me for a few moments with her almost unfathomable dark eyes. I saw pride there. She was proud of me.

"Honor your abilities Marc, but it would be wise not to mention them to others," she said. "That way your gifts remain pure and untainted by the attitudes of people who may not understand you."

I was only seven years old. She reached out and put her hands on my shoulders and kissed me on the forehead. She was not an affectionately expressive kind of person—even with me. Thinking about that day years later the kiss seemed more like an initiation. I had stepped through the first door.

I believe that all people have gifts such as mine; abilities that rest more or less latent. I tip my hat to those who are aware of their talents and strive to nourish and utilize them.

My mother worked a clerical job in a small town nearby. She was a very private person–Saturnine–tall, dark, and elegant. Her native language was French, but being from Montreal she spoke English as well.

We lived very simply. The only luxury she reserved for herself was high quality tea. What was available locally was not acceptable to her, so twice a year we would make the journey, by bus, to the Pike Place Market in Seattle, where she would purchase a quantity of teas suitable to her palette. She drank tea daily from a tea set that I was not allowed to handle—even as a teenager. I didn't mind. I loved my mother with the pure untainted love of a child.

The depth of what a child perceives and knows can be astounding, considering their lack of experience. Much of that simple clarity of mind is inevitably burned away by the fires of puberty, and replaced by a kind of arrogant blindness. Our memories of those days however, remain. We peer back through a small, dusty window as we strive to regain that purity, exuberance, and natural healthiness which we were once graced.

There were days when I was hungry, but I tried not to let my mother know it. They were simpler times; when a young child could be left alone to fend for themselves at home for awhile when their parents were away. The older lady next door was supposed to keep an eye on me, but she would often be seen snoozing in the afternoon on her front porch.

At six years old I recall walking down the hill to the Three Tree Point store and sitting on the rough hewn planks underneath the log-cabin style hitching-post railing and eating an ice cream sandwich in the summer sun. The beach was close by, and it did not take me long to discover the old Indian trail, which went around the point above the beach a hundred feet or so. Today only a fragment of it remains, but in the 1930's it was over a mile long. Short sturdy bare feet had walked that trail for so many seasons that nothing grew on it; even in sections where bushes bent over it years later.

The Indians were gone, but there were still piles of clam shells and the remains of rotting longhouses as a testament to their sojourn in that place.

Years before Chief Sealth had said:

"Every part of this soil is sacred in the estimation of my people. Every hillside, every valley, every plain and grove, has been hallowed by some sad or happy event in days long vanished. Even the rocks, which seem to be dumb and dead as they swelter in the sun along the silent shore, thrill with memories of stirring events connected with the lives of my people, and the very dust upon which you now stand responds more lovingly to their footsteps than yours, because it is rich with the blood of our ancestors, and our bare feet are conscious of the sympathetic touch. Our departed braves, fond mothers, glad, happy hearted maidens, and even the little children who lived here and rejoiced here for a brief season, will love these somber solitudes and at eventide they greet shadowy returning spirits. And when the last Red Man shall have perished, and the memory of my tribe shall have become a myth among the White Men, these shores will swarm with the invisible dead of my tribe, and when your children's children think themselves alone in the field, the store, the shop, upon the highway, or in the silence of the pathless woods, they will not be alone. In all the earth there is no place dedicated to solitude. At night when the streets of your cities and villages are silent and you think them deserted, they will throng with the returning hosts that once filled them and still love this beautiful land. The White Man will never be alone."

"Let him be just and deal kindly with my people, for the dead are not powerless. Dead, did I say? There is no death, only a change of worlds."

They watched me as I padded down the trail in my bare feet with a bucket and a garden spade. I learned to gather food much like the Indians had. The barnacles and shells on the beach were sharp, but from day one I preferred to hunt barefoot, like my predecessors and silent mentors had years before.

I became a clam digger.

Unlike razor clams and geoducks, butter clams cannot flee from predators quickly, and are easy prey—even for a child. I learned by my own industry how not to be hungry. I would lug the heavy bucket of dollar-sized pungent clams home and present them to my mother, who would steam them or make a chowder. At first she was alarmed that I had ventured out so far, but the second time I brought them home bits of tears welled up in her eyes. My actions were an admittance of my hunger. She was proud that her little son was bringing food home for the table, but frustrated that she had not been able to feed me more.

I gained in power. If I was hungry, I could do something about it. Eventually I went for the big game: the Silver, Sockeye, and Chinook salmon that ran around the point in their seasons.

One year she gave me a bamboo fishing pole and a surf-casting reel for my birthday. In those days a gift like that was expensive. She must have saved all year for it.

I would perch on what remained of an old ferry dock and cast out into the deep water, with the cold, nuptial waves swelling under my feet. I caught more cod and flounder than salmon that way, but it was all good food.

At the age of eleven I joined a local boy scout troop; which would probably be better described as a squad than a troop, with about five boys and two scout masters.

The two men were best friends, and shared a passion for the alpine slopes of nearby Mt. Rainier.

One of the men had a big Oldsmobile with a rumble seat. We strapped our gear onto the running boards, piled in and headed up towards Mt. Rainier National Park.

Once we entered the park the roads were new, due to in part by the work done by the Civilian Conservation Corps; an organization created by President Roosevelt to help men that were out of work. The CCC had built low stone walls along the freshly paved asphalt roads, which along with the breathtaking natural beauty of the place created an impression of sanctity and majesty.

After driving between cedar and fir trees the size of houses, we stopped at Longmire lodge to eat lunch at a picnic table and drink water from a spring that bubbled out of the ground nearby.

The Longmire resort had existed prior to the creation of Mt. Rainier National Park. The water that came out of the ground there was believed to have healing properties. In the 1890's, tourists in wagons and on horseback had braved the rutted, muddy roads so that they could lounge in the sulfur and iron baths.

My first experience drinking it left no doubt that there was some truth to the remarkable quality of the water there. One of the scoutmasters was a big fan of it. He led us a hundred feet down the trail that circles the springs to an unimpressive pool surrounded by a few stones. There he eagerly filled his canteen and proceeded to take a huge draught of it. I tried it. The water was effervescent, with a curious round taste. As we walked back to the picnic table, I began to feel electrical shocks, like tiny pin pricks all over my skin, accompanied by little white flashes of light in my field of vision. The sensation was agreeable, not to mention unusual. Later in the day, when I again drank more of it from the canteen, it failed to produce the same reaction. Why remains a mystery, but later I discerned that the water must be fresh to produce a noticeable reaction.

That day we camped by a lake in the meadows. The wildflowers of all colors were in full bloom. Some were waist high, with baseball-sized spherical seed heads that looked like pompoms as they swayed in the gentle breeze.

The fragrance of alpine areas is peculiar. All life that thrives there, from huge elk down to the tiniest bacteria are all highly active for only a brief time in late summer. The large mammals may move elsewhere during the winter, but the smaller, indigenous creatures and plants must feed and produce offspring or seeds in a few short weeks before their long winter hibernation. The air teems with pollen, the fragrance of flowers and the resins of conifers: spruces, alpine firs, and yellow cedars. Communally they produce a unique natural perfume—eau d'alpine.

Our scoutmasters were good teachers, and traded off sharing their knowledge of mountaineering skills with us. Boys of that age are rambunctious, which gave the men some time to themselves. At the end of the day the two friends climbed up to a rock where they could smoke their pipes, watch the sunset, and keep an eye on us at the same time.

2

Airborne

I graduated from high school in 1941 and immediately went to work for the Boeing aircraft company. While much of the rest of the world was at war, American companies responded by accepting contracts to supply massive amounts of wartime goods. The list of countries ordering supplies was long: England, Australia, and China were just a few. The Soviet Union ordered a million pairs of boots, blankets and Studebaker trucks. America, with it's seemingly unlimited natural resources and a huge, willing labor force went to work.

After the attack on Pearl Harbor in 1942, America declared war on Japan and it's Axis allies. The Boeing company became a strategic target and feared being bombed by the Japanese air force. I worked on the design team with the carpenters to create a mock housing development directly on top of Boeing's production plant south of Seattle. From the air, it was designed to look like houses, roads, and trees. The only telltale sign that it was an aircraft production facility were the B-17 "Flying Fortresses" we were building that were lined up every day on nearby Boeing field ready for delivery.

Since I worked in what was determined a "critical industry", I was not conscripted until early in 1943.

The pull for young men to go to war is strong. By the time I was drafted, most of the able-bodied young men I knew were already serving. I had been glad to be helping with the war effort by building airplanes, but when my time came I volunteered for parachute duty with the U.S. Army.

After basic training I was sent to Camp Toccoa in the backwoods of Georgia for paratrooper evaluation. The officer in charge was Lt. Colonel Louis A. Walsh Jr. Most of the soldiers that passed the psychological and rigorous physical tests were sent off to the 17th Airborne Division or elsewhere in the army, but Colonel Walsh cherry-picked the most promising applicants for his own unit. It was called the 517th Parachute Regimental Combat Team, and was essentially Walsh's baby. He had experienced some tough fighting in the south Pacific and was determined to create a small, well trained fighting force.

Colonel Walsh insisted on very high standards. To remain in the 517th, every soldier had to qualify as "expert" with his weapon, "sharpshooter" with another, and "marksman" with other weapons in the platoon. By modern standards, the 517th would be considered a special forces group.

Somehow I qualified and was soon given the rank of corporal probably because I was a couple of years older than most of the recruits. On May 17th, 1944 we boarded the Santa Rosa liner destined for Naples, Italy.

We saw some action in Italy, and then became part of the initial attack force in the successful invasion of southern France called "Operation Dragoon" on the 15th of August.

One night two "sticks" of soldiers were loaded aboard two C-47 airplanes for a clandestine drop into eastern France deep behind the German lines. We were accompanied by two OSS officers—one for each plane. We were not told anything about our mission, except that once on the ground we were to group and receive instructions from the OSS officers.

The OSS was later to become the CIA.

I was the last soldier to jump out of our plane. We had been encountering quite a bit of turbulence. Daryl Baker, my buddy from New Hampshire, went out right before me.

"See you on the ground Marc!"

"Okay Daryl!"

I never saw any of those guys again, and never learned what became of them. The movements of the 517th in Italy and France have been well documented by military historians, but there has been no mention of our drop into the Jura mountains between France and Switzerland on that early morning in August of 1944.

I am a sword in a sheath of darkness
My once proud edge rests idle, silently corroding,
Ignoring its latent prowess
The jewels in my pommel have no luster without
The light
The engraving in my handle is lost to the blackness
The darkness is my ally—the night my friend
There is safety in the embrace of the night
Enveloped in the womb of soft blackness
I feel no sorrow—no pain
In total blackness I am free
Free to roam through time and space
Free of this tedious world
I have no use for the light
I am wed to the shadows
The speed of light?
What is the speed of darkness?
Much faster I tell you
The light is a fair-weather friend
Darkness is eternal

3

Descent

Ajolt of turbulence knocked me backwards, delaying my jump.

The C-47's crewman helped me up. "Lets go soldier. You don't want to be late for the party!"

I hurled myself into the cold blackness. When my parachute opened I was immediately hit by a gust or an updraft and pushed sideways. Wind conditions in mountain areas can be violent and unpredictable. My chute luffed as I continued to move sideways for what seemed like a long time. I was struggling to keep my parachute full when the moon peeked out from between the clouds. Looking down, I didn't understand what I saw. The world underneath my feet had divided into two halves—black and white, with the dividing line directly below. It looked like an alien world, or perhaps the very edge of our own.

Precisely at the black and white line my boots plunged into the snow before lifting off again and heading down into the darkness. I was blind in the blackness, but I realized where I had briefly landed—on a ridge at the very peak of a mountain. The moon had chosen to illuminate the snow on one side only.

My feet dug through the crust into the soft snow again and I tumbled down the impossibly steep slope, wrapped up in the parachute like a silkworm in its cocoon. I hit a cornice hard and became airborne for what was probably only a split second, but it seemed like a long time. It is amazing what my mind went through in less time than it takes to breath one breath. I thought that was it—I was history, and would plummet to my death alone on that unyielding mountain. When I landed the slope was not as steep, and I swiveled around so my feet went down first and jammed my gun barrel through the fabric into the snow on my left side to arrest my fall, and at the same time tried to dig the heels of my heavy paratrooper boots into the snow.

On one of our scouting excursions to Mt. Rainier, we had rented ice axes at Paradise lodge and practiced "glissading" down the steep, wet snowfields in the same manner. Here, high in the Jura mountains I managed to slow my descent enough so that when I slammed into the rocks at the bottom of the glacier I was bruised, but unharmed.

I lay there for a minute listening to the gurgling sound of water, reveling that I was still alive. Finally I cut myself free of the parachute and tangled cords with my bayonet. Standing up I could barely see a little copse of short alpine trees nearby. In the dark they looked like gnarled mountain gnomes—beckoning to me to enter their chilly subterranean world. I did, and found a nest of dead branches in amongst them I could bivouac on until the sun came up. I wrapped back up in the parachute and did just that. There was no sleep however—it was much too cold.

Somewhere I had heard that you can create a fire of warmth around your body with your mind. I tried that for awhile, and for a time it seemed to work, but then I ended up shivering for three long hours until it became light enough to see. When the twilight finally made its presence known, I felt that I wasn't really in a hurry. I could just lay there for awhile and think about things.

Then I remembered that apathy was a prime symptom of hypothermia. There are times when we find that we are stronger than we know. My body did not want to move, but I willed it to do so—slowly and methodically.

I believe that my boy scout training gave me enough insight about the dynamics of alpine areas to save my life that frigid morning on the pediment of that glacier which towered in the twilight above eastern France.

I slowly and carefully gathered firewood. One of the gnome-trees was dead, so became a sacrifice to my survival. I collected the driest pieces by snapping off dead branches and made three piles of different sizes. I did not smoke but carried a lighter anyway, which became another sacrifice. I lit it, placed it into a hollow and covered it with the driest, smallest branches. Fortunately there was no wind in the early morning. The fire was not large enough to fully warm me, but I managed to produce a canteen full of warm water, and in the coals heat up a tin of Spam. I drank the almost-hot water and ate the strange-smelling Spam. Warm liquid is the key to reviving a person suffering from hypothermia.

Without lingering, I packed-up and headed down through the fog, following the stream. I knew *it* knew where it was going—downhill. I was still almost too cold to walk. My hands were cold, my feet were cold, my head was cold. I was geared for summer fighting, not mountaineering. I picked my way downhill for a few hours. When the sun finally made its appearance and began to displace the fog it was dramatic, and somewhat of a revelation. The muted grays of the wildflowers became transformed into shocking pinks, indigo blues, deep purples, scarlets, yellows and bright snowy whites.

When the fog fully lifted I found myself standing in a large descending meadow that was, in its moment, one of the most beautiful places on earth. It was teeming with wildflowers. Even though I was still quite cold, I couldn't help but stop and marvel at the pristine beauty of it. A group of wildflowers watched me as I drank some of the water. I put my parachute bundle against a cream-colored rock next to the stream and leaned back on it for a while, catching a bit of warmth from the sun.

I was in a jungle area and being cautiously approached by a black jaguar—a female. I was frightened as she slowly padded up and sniffed at me. She then turned and allowed herself to be stroked in the manner of cats. I did so lightly, aware of the formidable power of the animal. She continued to appear and reappear throughout the rest of the dream; observing and accompanying me from a distance.

When I awoke the wildflowers were still watching me. I spent some time inspecting and cleaning my weapon.

It was a brutal thing I had done to it; using it as an ice ax. The stock was a little loose and the end of the barrel was scratched from dragging it over the rocks, but it appeared functional.

I continued to follow the stream down hill, ignoring the game trails. Animals have their own reality. Their trails meander from food source to water source and have little meaning for us. Few of them made an appearance except for a little viper and a deer in the distance. The viper surprised me. There were no poisonous snakes where I came from, and certainly not in the alpine areas.

The meadows were broad and open with rolling, well rounded hills. These mountains were much older than the rugged Cascade range I was familiar with. Geology and time had managed to smooth and soften them.

For the most part it was a pleasant stroll downhill, except for a short cliff that I tried to traverse—with no luck. I finally had to lower myself down over it with some of the parachute cord. We were supposed to abandon our chutes but the thing was still proving useful, so I carried it in a bundle beneath my pack.

Towards the end of the day, as I descended into the sub-alpine forest the wildflowers gradually gave way to more trees and bushes. I decided to set up camp early, well before the sun went down. I built a small open-sided shelter with the parachute in amongst some trees near the stream. Determined to stay warm, I collected a huge pile of firewood.

Most of it was light and half rotten, having laid there for years. But kept me warm it did, as I watched the old, fragrant, crystallized spruce sap liquefy and boil out of the ends of branches and drip into the heart of the fire.

It is interesting what the mind will do in the dark with no one to talk to and nothing to do. The orange embers of the fire become the focal point—mesmerizing like a mandala. I thought about the black jaguar dream. It almost seemed like a visitation from a totem animal, like in American Indian lore—A protector spirit.

Eventually I succumbed to the sleep of exhaustion.

When I awoke in the early morning the fire was out and clouds had moved in. The going became tougher as I continued to follow the stream downhill. It went through an entire gamut of its manifestations as the grade became steeper. It would meander through a hollow, become a waterfall as it tumbled over a rock, pause as it rested in a pool after the tumultuous fall, then finally continue onward. I drank plenty of water.

After falling down steep slopes and through dense underbrush for hours, the stream went over a short cliff. I climbed down to a flat spot on the cliff from where I thought I could cross the stream and make a traverse off to the left. The landing was larger than it appeared from above, and had a curious feel to it. It was early afternoon and beginning to rain. When I backed up to take shelter under the overhang, I realized that there was an opening in the cliff wall blocked by the only bush that tenaciously grew on the rock landing. The bush made entry difficult, but I managed to push it aside enough to squeeze through the opening.

A twenty-one year old man is only nine years removed from being a twelve-year-old boy, who cannot pass up an opportunity to investigate a cave. In fact, discovering caves is one of the unspoken duties of all boys worldwide, who willingly perform the task with relish.

The cave was small, but easily large enough for a person to sleep in, with a relatively flat floor of hard-packed earth. The twelve-year-old part of me was pleased to make the conquest, so I decided to rest there and wait-out the rain squall. As my eyes adjusted to the dark, I could see that the place had in fact been used for shelter or habitation long before. Near the opening the roof was blackened by fire; and in the back of the cave faint paintings, and odd symbols had been drawn on the walls. The place was positively Neolithic. The bush blocking the opening was decades old. It was unlikely the cave had received visitors during its life.

An hour passed before the rain stopped and the sun blared out. I made the traverse to the south, and after battling with some thick bushes came into a more open spruce forest. Looking back uphill, I wondered how one would find that cave again. You would really have to know it was there.

Presently I came to a forest road. A road junction was nearby. Worn pointer signs with French place names on them hung on a weathered post. The only name I recognized was Geneva, which was directed towards the road going uphill. I chose to head back towards the stream, which by road wasn't far. It flowed under the road through a heavy copper pipe. Looking uphill, I estimated that the cave I had taken refuge in was perhaps only two or three hundred yards upstream.

I heard the sound of a vehicle approaching. There was a rough, uneven track on the downhill side of the road. I ducked down it a ways and hid behind a tree. Two vehicles passed: a car and an open truck filled with German soldiers.

I noticed that there was a structure further down
the track. It was a small cabin, or cottage really, in that
it was made of stone, with a crumbling thatch roof.
I approached quietly, and investigated with my gun barrel. It was vacant. The narrow entry door was too low
for me to pass without stooping, and had what appeared
to be a thick, twisted root mortared in as a header. A
small stone palette had been built into the wall, opposite a crude fireplace with an iron pot hanging off of a
hook inside. The only furniture was a small, heavy table
blackened with use, and the remains of it's accompanying bench, which lay crumbled on the floor. There was
only one narrow window—facing back, that looked like
it had been retrofitted with a piece of glass many years
before. Next to it was another ancient door. It was falling
off of it's rusted hinges, which looked as if they had been
hammered out of a pre-historic forge.

My first thought was that it was a hunter's cabin.
However, it had more of the appearance of a monks cell.
It bore a kind of undefinable resemblance to the cave I
had rested in upstream.

It was late afternoon. The cottage could provide me
with shelter, but the stone palette looked uncomfortable,
and it was not a good defensive position; so I headed off
down the road.

The further I went the more nervous I became, for
two reasons: One was that there was absolutely no cover.
I was walking on a mountain road, with a cliff above
and a steep drop off below. I began to move faster down
the road, at a slow measured trot, hoping to get past the
area. It was also beginning to rain again. Dark ominous
clouds were approaching from the valley below.

I came to a ruined chateau—an obvious casualty of the war. Noticing some steps that remained intact going down into a cellar I investigated. It was dark underground, but the cellar appeared to be about ten feet wide and had been dug into the hill thirty feet or so. It was difficult to tell due to the debris: wine bottles scattered on the floor and barrels piled up in the back. It was an even worse defensive position than the cottage. I could be caught like a rat in a trap down there, but it was dry, so I put the parachute bundle against a wall near the steps and sat down, leaning up against it.

I watched the big rain drops as they pelted off of the steps for a few minutes. Then I heard a scuffling sound coming from the back of the cellar—too big for a rat. Alarmed, I jumped up with my weapon and cautiously moved back there. My eyes had partially adjusted to the dark, and what I saw frightened me: a white face hovering in the blackness. It reminded me of one of those horror movies with that creepy Bella Lagosi playing *Dracula*. My gun barrel was inches from the face when the eyes blinked. My heart was beating too fast. I came to my senses and lowered my weapon.

It was the face of a woman.

"I am sorry I didn't..."

I was in France. The two years of French language I had studied in high school was not enough to provide me with conversational skills. I only knew a few phrases and vocabulary. My pronunciation was good however, due to some coaching from my mother.

"Pardonnez-moi Madame. Je m'appelle Marc—American."

I waited. No response, just that face staring at nothing.

I pulled out my last bit of food, a crumbled Hersheys bar, and offered a piece to her.

"Chocolate Madame?"

Still no response—only another blink. I was not going to venture out into the rain. She would just have to be stuck with me for awhile. I pointed to the floor where I had been sitting. "S'il-vous-plaît?" She had no choice. I sat down and rested against the parachute bundle again.

I awoke to the sound of brakes squealing, a transmission being crammed into reverse, and a woman urgently speaking in French.

"Monsieur! Monsieur!...Allez...Allez!"

She was beckoning to me as I jumped up, grabbed my pack, threw it behind a barrel, and went back into the cellar to hide near her, tucking behind an old rough post. I could see through a hole in the bricks where the mortar had crumbled away.

The tip of a rifle barrel appeared, followed by a wet German soldier wearing an overcoat. He swore softly as he fumbled with a flashlight that kept blinking on and off. Fortunately for me, his investigation of the cellar wasn't very thorough. He was still messing with the flashlight when a command-question baritoned down from up above. The soldier replied, and an officer came down the stairs. He produced the stub of a candle, lit it and set it on a shelf. The colonel was a big man with a broad Germanic face, and a ski-jump nose. He surveyed the room for a moment from where he was standing. They went back up the stairs and came down lugging a heavy wooden crate, which they set against the wall across from where I had been sitting. They both then looked up the stairs.

The first I saw of the other officer were his boots: shiny, black, high quality, knee-high leather boots. They paused on the third step down, then proceeded quickly, realizing that the pause had mistakenly displayed a weakness. Even before he removed his oilskin I knew he was an SS officer because of his hat: black with silver trim. German officers' uniforms were already slick, but the SS officer's attire was of a different order. It was *tailored* to fit him perfectly, and designed to make a statement: I am elite, ruthless and dangerous.

He was a small man with dark, oily hair, beady brown eyes and a round red nose with creases on either side. He told the soldier to stand guard above. His voice was in the same high pitch range as the soldier's but was harsh, reedy—abrasive to the ear, in contrast to the younger man's melodic tenor. The order was important, formal, and had an unmistakable *or else* attached to it. I suspected that *every* command uttered by the SS officer was an important one.

He was the kind of man whose schoolmates had administered regular beatings to, simply because he was small, ugly, and had a generally irritating demeanor. Children may be angelic at times, but they also can be cruel and animalistic. The weak must be eliminated so that the strong will have more food to survive. Girls humiliated him, and women ignored him. He responded by spending his adult life trying to punish and dominate others.

He produced a handkerchief, laid it on the wooden crate, and sat down on it. The regular army colonel sat down against the opposite wall. The SS officer pulled a flat silver flask out of his lapel, took a drink out of it, then offered it to the other officer.

It was a completely hollow gesture. The colonel pulled out his own flask and held it up in response. As they were toasting to the Fuhrer, I got a clear truth picture:

They were basically of the same rank, but the SS officer was in charge and the colonel resented it. He had a strong dislike for the little man, but disciplined himself not to show it. Crossing an SS officer could mean hardship or death to oneself and one's family. The colonel considered him nothing more than a murderer in fancy clothes; a politician who had scratched and clawed his way into a position of power.

The SS officer knew that the colonel didn't like him, but didn't care. The colonel was the kind of man he had struggled with all of his life; a big, plodding man from a privileged family. He considered the other man's antipathy as a weakness; one to be exploited. He was in the habit of using other's dislike of him to his advantage.

They both pulled out cigarettes, and began smoking in silence. The gray-blue smoke began to fill the room. I was glad because it provided me with more visual cover, but I then realized that I had to urinate—badly. My bladder felt like it was going to burst. I had been on a steady diet of spring water for two days, had slept for an hour, and been awakened hastily. I tried to ignore it, but that of course made it worse. I could not crouch in that uncomfortable position all night without making a sound, nor could I shoot the two officers when the soldier was above. All he would have to do is toss a grenade into the cellar. I had seen one on his belt.

Two things then happened at once: The SS officer began staring at the parachute bundle I had left against the wall in haste, and the dripping, wet soldier came down the stairs and asked the SS officer for a cigarette.

I thought the soldier must be a little daffy to approach him like that, but the officer ignored him, focusing on the bundle. The regular army colonel—used to taking care of his men, handed the soldier a cigarette, and began to help him light it.

It was my opportunity, but I realized that my weapon still had the safety button on after bushwhacking through the forest. Between my thumb and finger I tried to slide the safety into the off position quietly, but it still made an audible click. The sound of a safety switch is one that every soldier knows well.

The SS officer uncoiled like a snake, pulled out his pistol and hastily squeezed off a shot.

My weapon was a Thompson, coveted by many U.S. servicemen. The Tommy-gun was not particularly effective in long-range battle situations, but was formidable in close quarters. It was capable of pumping out a pound of fat lead bullets in less than two seconds.

The candle flickered briefly, shining yellow through the dust kicked up by the excitement in the room. Perhaps the candle also shines on other higher plains of existence, paying little heed to, or completely unaware of the suffering of men. Maybe what we see of the flame is but a small part of the candle's being; merely its physical manifestation in our corporeal world.

I mechanically replaced the spent magazine with another and waited, my ears ringing, for the dust to settle. Finally, I got up and walked over to the young soldier, ignoring the officers. I really didn't want to kill that boy. His face staring up into the candlelight has haunted me to this day. I have felt a void of remorse for the other men that I killed in France. Somehow it all seemed to manifest in that one young soldier. He was but a pawn in that ugly war. Later, when I searched their bodies for money, I made the mistake of looking at the tiny photo of his sweetheart; a pretty girl with dimples and blond braids. I believe that the guilt from that experience is at the root of my present illness.

I stepped over the soldier, went up the stairs and relieved myself on the other side of the road. It was dark and the rain had ceased. The insects and frogs were making quite a hubbub that billowed up from the valley below. The automobile they had arrived in was one of those long, low German staff cars.

Many soldiers would have simply walked away from the scene, leaving it for the locals to clean up, but I felt responsible. The lady in the cellar had warned me. I dragged the young soldier up the stairs and muscled the body into the back seat, and did the same with the SS officer. When I went back down for the colonel I noticed that one of my bullets had torn across the wooden strongbox lid at an unnatural angle, shredding fresh hardwood splinters towards the wall. Through the jagged opening I spied the unmistakable glint of gold. I reacted calmly. I must have been in a kind of state of shock due to the fact that I had just killed three men; an act that would have been termed "cold blooded" if we had not been at war. Is there a difference? War or no war—my blood is not cold.

I rolled the strongbox up the stairs sideways, stood it up on its end behind the car and tilted it into the trunk. The colonel's body was too awkward and heavy for me to get up the stairs. I thought of asking the woman to help, but panicked for a moment because I realized I didn't know where the SS officer's bullet had landed.

I hurried into the back of the cellar and up to her. She was looking down at the floor.

"Comment allez-vous?"

She looked up and nodded her head—yes.

I pointed towards the stairs and gestured. She must have observed me struggling with the colonel. "I need help," I said.

She understood. When she got up and moved into the candlelight I saw why she had first appeared as only a spooky face. She was dressed in black from head to toe, with a scarf wrapped tightly around her head. She even had black ladies evening gloves tucked into the sleeves of her sweater. She didn't look up at me, but as she was brushing herself off I got a little truth picture:

She's a widow. Her husband had died earlier in the war, but not because of it. There was something disturbing about it all.

We dragged the colonel up the stairs and managed to get him into the front passenger seat. The widow then walked right back down into the cellar. I watched her go. I knew what she was doing. When I went back down for the last time to grab the SS officer's pistol off of the floor, she had returned to her corner.

I drove past the track to the cottage and found a cliff to dump the bodies off. First, I used the headlights to search them. I took the pistol belt, their wallets, an envelope the SS officer carried, the SS pin off of his collar, and the strongbox key out of one of his pockets. I knew where to look for that. I then drove back down to the cottage track and forced the car over it, parking in front of the building.

I removed a wool blanket out of the trunk I had seen and promptly laid down on the stone palette, but remained awake for a long time in the dark.

In the morning I had a flying dream. I was aware that I was dreaming. It had been a long time since I had flown in a dream. It felt so good that I spread my arms out, tilted my head back and flew straight upwards—Yes!

The dream produced an emotion strong enough to wake me up. The sun was out and the birds were singing. I thought about the dream and listened to the birds. The birds still sing; regardless of what we do. The idea reminded me of the possibility of the candle burning in another reality.

The presence of the wool blanket re-assured me that the events of the previous day had, in fact occurred. I went out and opened the trunk of the car, and unlocked the padlock. The strongbox was filled with gold coins wrapped in paper tubes. On top of the coins was a thin rectangular metal case. I moved that aside and pawed through the coins. As far as I could tell they were all the same type of coins, but from different years. They were French gold coins—slightly smaller than American silver dollars, with a gorgeous rendition of an angel on the face of each. I grabbed the metal case, one of the coins and shut the lid. I noticed a tin of sardines back further in the trunk. When I reached for it my stomach growled. I almost laughed out loud at the absurdity of it all. What is more important right now? A tin of sardines or a pot-of-gold? I went inside and ate the sardines.

After I'd finished my snack, I put all of my booty out on the table for me to peruse. I propped the door open with my weapon so I could see and hear outside, and to let some light in. I needed time to think about what to do. The presence of the gold altered the situation dramatically.

I first examined the pistol. I liked the idea of carrying a sidearm, and this one was a handy, medium-sized semi-automatic. I cut the "Nazi" shoulder strap off of the gun belt and strapped it around my waist western-style.

I then tried to read the orders the SS officer had been carrying. As far as I could tell, the orders were the typical rhetoric and mentioned few specifics. The presence of the gold was a secret. I saved the orders, with the intention to present them to headquarters later.

The thin metal case seemed to be made of a soft, non-corrosive metal, probably tin. Inside was a brown leather envelope tied with a strap. The envelope contained a piece of parchment, with writing on it in what appeared to be Latin. I had never handled parchment, but I assumed that's what it was because it was crinkly and uneven in texture. Towards the bottom of the page something that looked like my name was written on it. That made no sense at all. I didn't know what to make of it so I returned it to it's case and dropped it behind a board in the wall.

I must have sat there for about an hour rolling the gold coin around in my hand and looking out the door. I may have been young, but I was not naive. If I turned the gold in to the proper "authorities" it would quickly end up secretly filling the coffer of some clever person's safety deposit box. I thought of the sign up the road that pointed to Geneva, and began to formulate a plan. I would survive this war.

I liked the lines of the German car. I hid it in one place and the gold in another.

4

The Return

That afternoon I found myself trotting down the road again. When I got to the ruined château I ducked in to see if the widow was all right. I somehow felt responsible for the events the previous evening. *The black jaguar came into my mind.*

"Madame? Je suis Marc...American. Comment allez-vous?"

No answer. I went further into the cellar. There was still a face there, hovering in the darkness.

I said it in English, because I could express it with more passion. "I just wanted to see if you were all right."

The tone was kind and sincere—still no response. *She was just going to starve huddling in there.* There must be some place she could go? I became insistent.

"Madame...comment allez-vous?"

The eyes blinked, and she spat out a sentence too fast for me to understand.

"Pardonnez-moi, je ne comprends pas. Lentement s'il-vous-plaît?" I said.

She understood, huffed and said it slower. *Good—I had a dialogue going.* This time I got it. She was asking

31

me where the three Germans were. I pointed up the road. She blinked twice, and spat out another quick sentence, huffed again, then said it slower. Where did I sleep?

I didn't know quite what to call the place.

"Uh...le petite château?" I pointed up the road again.

She quickly jumped up and brushed past me—stumbling at the doorway. She didn't have her legs after sitting for so long. She climbed the stairs and began marching up the road.

I followed, and burdened with all of my gear struggled to keep up with her. When I had almost caught up with her I heard the unmistakable sound of a truck engine coming up the road. She stopped—I looked around. There was absolutely no cover. There was a steep drop-off down below and an embankment on the other side of the mountain road. I jumped off the edge of the road, found a footing and clung on to a root. "Madame?"

She looked down at me, down the road, hesitated, then scrambled in next to me. She couldn't find a good footing, so I grabbed her around her waist and held tight. It was not a hiding place. The passenger in a vehicle could simply look down and see us. The driver might even be able to. The truck rumbled past us. It was German. The soldier in the passenger seat was asleep, his helmet pressed against the window. As it passed, I saw soldiers in the back of the truck, and had eye contact with one of them. I know he saw me, because his eyes moved as they drove on, but he did not move. He looked exhausted beyond exhaustion. I recognized "the look"—that blank stare of soldiers that have witnessed more gore, guts, and inhumanity than any sensitive person ever should.

Whatever war, whatever time, whatever nation; those soldiers become scarred beyond normal functionality in a society, and live out the rest of their lives hiding in their own angry world, perpetually wary of the dangers that are out there lurking beyond their gates.

The German truck passed without incident.

We both breathed a sigh of relief. I know—I felt her do it. We looked at each other and shared a moment— just a second, but it was enough. *We did it!.*

It was the first time I had really got a good look at her. We were almost nose to nose. She was younger than I had thought—about my age. Her face was narrow, oval, with high cheekbones, olive skin, brown eyes with a tinge of green (like mine), and her nose was long and curved, flattening at the tip—very French; perhaps a bit too large for most American women.

In her own unique way, she was the most exotic, beautiful woman I had ever seen.

She recoiled and scrambled up onto the road.

With all of my gear, try as I might, I couldn't climb up out of there. I still had the parachute tied in a bundle, my pack, and weapon. The edge of the road was rounded with no hand hold. I called up the road after her.

"Madame...Madame, s'il-vous-plaît?"

The feisty vixen turned and looked at me. Annoyed, she came back down, grabbed the back of my pack, and helped me get up onto the road. I didn't catch up with her then. After half a kilometer, she turned right towards the cottage and headed down the track. By the time I got there, I had realized what she was doing. She was very protective of this place and was concerned that I had left the bodies of the German soldiers there. She looked inside the building, then went through it into the back.

I reassured her that the bodies were not there.

The cottage was built on a solid rock outcropping, with a break in the trees that looked out to the valley below. The little creek ran through the back, and rolled over the cliff. Before it disappeared, it flowed through a small pool. The rock had been carved in such a way as to create a spiral effect—a miniature whirlpool in constant motion. I knelt down, filled my canteen and drank deeply. She eyed me curiously.

When I drank the water, I realized how hungry I was and had an idea. *It seemed like every time I drank that water I thought of something.* I stood up, pulled out one of the bills that I had filched off of the Germans, and held it out to her. It was French money. I wanted to ask her to buy food, but I didn't know how to say it. "J'ai faim. Du pain, du fromage, un fruit s'il- vous-plaît?" She understood, turned and looked out into the valley. I sat down on the stone bench holding the open canteen.

It was then that I realized how beautiful the place was. There was nothing modern about it. We could have been in any time, with the rock outcropping and forest opening roughly framed by the oak branches looking out towards the valley bathed in the sun below. Dressed in black, she could have been a Delphic oracle from ancient Greece. Statuesque—Stunning. She was struggling with some- thing. I had been nothing but courteous and kind to her. We were alone, and another soldier may have behaved in a much less gentlemanly fashion. She turned her head and looked at me compassionately. *So she wasn't totally vixen after all.* Besides, she had to be hungry. I had held my arm around her waist. She was skin and bones.

He had not defiled the sanctuary. The fact that he had found it at all—and used it was intriguing. As he knelt by the fairy pool and drank, a bit of soft yellow light surrounded his body as the water energized him. Those kind eyes had unnerved her. The eyes were set up and behind flat spots on the inside of the cheek bones. Severity and beauty. They were the eyes of an idealist— a mystic; One who has a vision of a finer world, and therefore struggles with the crudeness of this one. He was however, one mystic with talons and a beak as she had observed the night before. He was certainly not the first warrior to find sanction here. There was the tale of a wounded Templar knight, fleeing from King Phillip's and the Pope's henchmen. It was he who had left the riddle inscribed on the wall in Old Latin.

No one but her had come here for as long as she could remember. This had been her sanctuary. She had spent the days alone, watching the fairies dance around the whirlpool. This is where, at the age of eleven, she'd had her first vision. Her body had just begun to change. The place was rife with stuffy old legends—musty like its crumbling thatch roof. She had not considered that a modern warrior could seek refuge here.

Perhaps the Templar had returned.

She stepped into the sun, to the left of the clearing, over a large rock and disappeared downhill. I was surprised, because I had a nose for trails and I hadn't seen that one. Still holding the money, I looked down over the cliff to see her traversing it directly below. She looked up and beckoned to me to accompany her.

It was more of a rocky goat trail, switching back and forth down towards the valley. Every time it crossed the stream, stones had been arranged in interesting ways at the crossings. We moved downhill in silence for some time. I had my weapon out, and stayed a good distance behind so as not to involve her in a skirmish. Eventually we came to a point in the stream where there was a larger pool and a standing stone, positioned like a shrine. When I got there she was kneeling, drinking water out of her hands. She stayed that way with her eyes closed for a minute, as if in prayer. When she was finished she told me to wait there.

Fifty yards below was a pond that was fed by the stream and flowed into the valley below. I saw it as an opportunity to quickly bath and launder my underclothes. I rushed through it, hung my underwear on a sunny rock and took up a defensive position. I needn't have hurried. She didn't return for over three hours. Finally I saw her lithe figure coming up the path. She was clean and had donned a fresh black dress.

She began speaking about a Monsieur and Madame Favreau. It seemed I had received an invitation to meet her aunt and uncle, who lived in the village below. When I understood, I agreed.

"Okay."

Her eyes twinkled.

"Oh-kee." Her mouth jutted outwards to form a little trumpet, and out of the tiny circle she pumped out the "O", and then her mouth did a complete reversal spreading wide into a flat pseudo-smile to produce the "kee".

She was mimicking me, and playing with the word. She had certainly seen Hollywood films. The wild American west had somehow captured the imagination of Europe's youth. She knew the expression, but this was the first time she had heard it directly out of the mouth of a genuine common American cowboy. I was a clam-digger not a cowboy, but I certainly wasn't going to pop her bubble now. She turned her head and moved down the trail.

The slope flattened out into fields of grass and wild-flowers; the trail becoming larger and following the stream closely. Eventually it led directly into the back yard of a tall, plain stone house. We walked through a little wooden gate, and I noticed how the stream had been funneled into a low stone fountain that splashed with soft gurgling sounds.

We were met by a short, compact lady with tightly rolled up blondish hair turning to gray. Her small blue eyes sized me up instantly. She barked a polite command to her niece, calling her "Céline". *That was her name.* It was something about dinner. The widow went inside. The lady then began speaking in excellent English, with a London/French accent.

"Thank you for bringing Céline here to us. We have been so worried about her. I am Madame Favreau, but you may call me Camille."

I wanted to back out of the responsibility of rescuing the widow, but it was indeed I who had coaxed her out of that cave.

"Thank you, I'm Marc Rémillard."

"Rémillard? An American with a noble French name."

"My parents were from Montreal."

"Were?"

"My father passed away before I was born."

"I see. I am sorry to hear that."

She reached over and quietly pulled the door shut.

"So...How did you find Céline?"

She was very direct and wanted an honest answer.

"I found her huddling in a corner in the cellar of that ruined château close to the road."

"That was her home. We looked for her there but could not find her."

"She was unresponsive when I first tried to talk to her. She was just staring blankly into space."

The lady looked down and let her breath out.

"Well, thank you again. Please come in."

She opened the door. The interior of the house was in sharp contrast to the plain outside. I could see fine, old carved wood furniture, and polished floors framing Iranian tribal rugs.

"I am afraid I cannot do that Madame. I am a soldier with these filthy boots and clothing."

I gestured down at my pants. They were in shreds from sliding down the snow field and bushwhacking through the forest. I had crudely lashed them together with bits of parachute cord. I looked like a beggar from the middle ages.

I perceived that I had earned brownie points for my politeness.

"Oh no, I insist. You can remove your boots. Xavier probably has a pair of trousers that no longer fit him. What is that you are carrying? Is that silk?"

"Yes, its my parachute."

"Parachute? Oh my!"

She fingered the dirty silk, admiring the quality.

"You can have it if you like Madame. I don't know why I am still carrying it."

She was pleased. I stepped inside and removed my boots.

Monsieur Favreau appeared. He was tall and dark like Céline. He did not speak English as well as his wife.

"Bonsoir Monsieur Favreau. Je m'appelle Marc Rémillard"

"Oh non...'Xavier' s'il-vous-plaît Marc."

He was very warm and friendly. Camille asked him to dress and clean me up for dinner. He took me in tow, helped me shave, loaned me a shirt, and gave me a pair of trousers that fit perfectly. They were the finest trousers I had ever worn, tailored out of a dense forest green corduroy. I was very glad I had chose to bathe in the pond.

5

The Dinner

It was one of those evenings that remains in ones memory, gradually attaining ever more significance as time passes. The golden gilding we envelope in an epic event can gain in thickness and luster, until it takes on the memorial ambiance of a Rembrandt painting: warm candlelight softly framed by darkness.

The experience was particularly poignant because of the contrast in realities. A mere day before I had been a ragged soldier of the mountains, and now I found myself in fine clothing, drinking wine, having dinner, and interesting conversations with my gracious hosts and the mysterious, lovely Céline.

We began the evening with cheese and white wine from Monsieur Favreau's vineyards. He was of course very proud of it. Tending to the vineyards was what occupied most of his time. He was particularly expressive, and more than willing to talk about the vines, the wines, or anything else inside his sphere of reality, which I gathered had become smaller with time. Even though he was less than sixty-five years old, he suffered from mild dementia, and tended to be forgetful. He freely told me that fact.

Madame Favreau was a superb host, making sure we had everything we needed, as well as smoothly steering the conversations toward amiable and productive topics. There was no question that it was she who powerfully grasped the rudder. At times Camille had to urge, or almost goad Céline into participating or helping; almost like a parent having to cajole a reluctant child into brushing their teeth or cleaning their room.

As I had been a wandering soldier the day before, Céline had been a crazy woman stubbornly huddling in a corner slowly wasting away. She could not be expected to be instantly chipper or chatty; two traits I suspected she had never expressed anyway. She did slowly eat well that evening—in spite of herself. She became interested in certain topics, while others elicited a staring-out-the window response. Anger and resentment seemed to be languishing just beneath a fragile calm surface.

While her aunt guided and directed Céline, her uncle was affectionate and fussed over her. The wine helped immensely. At first she refused to have any, but Xavier insisted. He was clever. He was seated to my right with Céline across from me. When she refused to drink his wine, he became deeply insulted. It was a blatant act— pure drama, which came close to actually getting a smile out of her. He had his right hand palm down on the table in front of her salad plate with the stem of a tall wine glass secured between two long sun-browned fingers. In his left hand he offered a horizontal bottle of his wine ready to pour.

"But Céline, you have not yet tried the 1942! I just opened the first bottle last week. It's the best yet—soft, but with plenty of fruit and crisp acidity." He looked over at me. "Céline has a superb palette." Then he turned back to her. "You must try it and tell me what you think!"

He went on about it until she relented. He poured a generous glass and leaned forward, impatiently awaiting for a response, ready to hang on every word.

He was irresistible. It was a marvelous performance. That evening I became an unwavering fan of Monsieur Xavier Favreau.

Camille and Xavier were a team. After we drank his wine, Camille brought out a special bottle of red wine from Bourgogne—what we call Burgundy. It turned out that both Camille and Céline favored the silky Burgundian reds, and this particular bottle was Céline's favorite. She knew what was going on, but marginally acquiesced, and as the evening progressed began to relax into the envelope of warmth and love of the couple.

They wanted to know how it was that I came to be there deep behind the German lines. When I began to relate what had happened I realized it was indeed a good story, even after omitting some important elements. For security reasons I could not tell them anything about my mission as a paratrooper, and for my own reasons did not mention the strongbox filled with gold coins or my hiding of the staff car.

They were surprised that I had found the stone hut, and impressed that I had slept there. They were particularly interested in the little stream that had served as both my guide and my nourishment. I assured them that it was in fact the same stream that flowed into their garden; the same stream I had used to navigate by down out of the mountains. They seemed to attach an unusual degree of importance to it.

When I asked why the stream had such significance, they demurred somewhat, but told me that the local people considered it a sacred spring. Apparently the standing stone was a kind of ancient shrine (no one knows how old) that had been used by pilgrims as a stop-over point for centuries.

When I expressed my respect for the profound beauty of the alpine areas I had passed through, Xavier responded with passion. He was also a lover of the upper meadows in their full glory in late summer, and had walked those paths as a younger man. He vowed to visit there again. I understood, because for me it could be considered a kind of pilgrimage that I must engage periodically.

They did not seem to relish in the killing of the German officers such as one would think French people might at that time. So I told them that the real reason I had killed those Germans was due to the fact that I had to urinate because I had been drinking so much of that wonderful water. That got a good chuckle out of them—even Céline, who was not privy to that particular detail, yet had been near me when I had pulled the trigger the evening before.

They were curious about my name. No one had ever shown any interest in it before. It was one of those non-English names that American school teachers struggle with the pronunciation of, and bullies make fun of.

Xavier questioned me. "Do you know anything about the Rémillard family?" He said it in the French way. I'd heard my mother use that pronunciation when speaking on the telephone. *Who had she been talking to?*

"No, except that my grandfather was Joseph Rémillard from Montreal."

44

"Your fathers father?"

"No, my mother's father..."

I had never put it together before. Then... *What was my father's name?*

Camille politely changed topics. They were interested in my family name for reasons that were unfathomable to me, but I perceived that they changed subjects because if I had been an illegitimate child it could be embarrassing for me. Was I?

Twice during the evening Xavier pointed to a photograph of a handsome young man that was displayed in the middle of the China cabinet, and announced proudly, "That is our son Jacques. He is an important member of the Prieuré de Sion!"

Camille and Céline stiffened.

I didn't know what he was referring to, but because of their reaction I politely asked no questions.

Sometime after that I became very tired and was having difficulty keeping my eyes open. Camille showed me to a room where I could sleep. I crawled between the thick, crisp, sun-dried sheets that gave off a hint of a floral fragrance. A real bed had never felt so luxurious.

The unicorn waits by the sacred spring. She knows he is coming. Her companions have fled into the forest. Nature is not afraid. Nature welcomes him and waits with her. She senses his approach even before she hears the beat of his wings. They are already allied in spirit, but must become so in flesh as well. She must join with the dragon—there at the sacred spring. Their offspring will be the hope of the world.

She has been the unicorn before. It is the ancient symbol of her family--once upon a time presented boldly on flags and emblazoned on the shields of men. In those days they were closely allied with the dragon clans.

The soldier had not been blown off course by the wind. The wind knew exactly what it was doing. It was only helping one who has misplaced the memory of who he is. He who yearns to fly. The device he uses is but a physical manifestation of an ability he already possesses. He has merely forgotten, and will learn to fly again. The mystic warrior is of the dragon clan.

She knew what she must do.

6

The Sacred Spring

I awoke early and found Madame Favreau drinking tea on the back patio. There was a cup and saucer, along with a light breakfast waiting for me on the other side of the table. As she reached out and poured me a cup of tea the low sun illuminated her from the back, turning her gray-blond hair into a little halo.

She was in a serious, contemplative mood.

After I had drank some of the tea she told me that two important things had occurred the night before. The first was that she had an important dream. I gathered that her dreams were her gift, much like my truth picture ability.

"I typically discuss my dreams freely, but I would like some time to think about this one first."

She eyed me curiously. "Céline has had a vision."

"A vision?"

"She has had them ever since she was a child. She would wake up sweating and sit up with her eyes open. They tend to be symbolic in nature. In those days she would tell us about them but now she keeps them as her own private experiences. We take them seriously."

Camille was being candid and challenging me to express disbelief in such matters—testing.

Processing the development I slowly nodded, accepted, held her gaze and drank more tea.

She relaxed a little. I was inside, not an outsider. She told me that they would like me to stay one more night if I was so inclined. I agreed.

After awhile I asked her if there was anything that I could do to help. She always needed fuel for the cook stove, so I ventured out to gather firewood. I had developed my own technique for bringing dry, dead branches down out of the trees that are much too high to reach. I tie a short heavy piece of branch to the end of a 30 foot cord, then spin and throw the stick like a sling up over a branch. When the stick twirls around the branch and temporarily locks into place, I pull down hard on the cord and break the branch off.

Madame Favreau was delighted when I brought my catch in: a massive pile of long branches I'd tied together with the cord and drug down the trail. An hour later I had them sawed into short lengths and stacked neatly for her. It was the least I could do.

I was cooling off in the shade with some lemonade at the back table when Céline appeared. Camille produced another glass of lemonade for Céline and left us alone. Céline sat upright and sipped some of the lemonade. She seemed nervous and distracted. We did not speak until she asked me if I would like to go up to the sacred spring. It was not really a request, and felt oddly formal. I could not refuse. She looked off to the side as I agreed.

Being that it was the hottest part of the day, after walking up the trail we were overheated. I took off my jacket and splashed some water on my face and head. I figured she must be hot—still dressed in black from head to toe. She removed the scarf from her head, and a pile of almost black lustrous hair billowed out from it. She reached out and grabbed a crude stone cup that rested at the base of the dolmen, plunged it into the pool, drank some of it, then offered the rest to me. As I was drinking she began to unbutton her dress. I thought she just needed to cool off until I noticed that her hands were shaking. Those shaking hands then began to unbutton my shirt. I finally realized what she was doing, and looked down at her hands struggling with the buttons. I reached up and gently grasped each trembling hand in mine. They were as beautiful as she was, with long slender fingers. She looked up at me, as if in thanks. I thought she was going to start crying, but she resumed her agenda, and after removing my shirt, she took off her underclothes and stood naked in front of me. By the time I took off my boxer shorts I was very excited. No woman had ever seen me like that.

She looked into my face, reached down and gently grabbed me.

I must admit that I had never been with a woman before. The super-beauties were often attracted to me, but I was much too shy to approach them. They usually ended up with the athletes or the slick operators. I had certainly never been touched like that by a woman. My mouth was hanging open. That got a smirk out of her. I think she realized that I was inexperienced.

She put her hands on my chest and pushed me down onto the mossy grass, climbed on top of me, and began the slow process of guiding me into her. The nervousness had been replaced by dedicated animation. She knew what she was doing. When I finally entered her she gasped, and began pushing harder. After that she was not in control—her body took over.

In my naivety I'd thought that men got what they wanted from women, who just tolerated it. This was quite the opposite: the savage need, the craving, the animal sounds. She was not giving to me; she was fiercely taking what she needed. It built into a crescendo of frantic movement, until she put her hands on my abdomen, sat up with her breasts pushed together between her arms and released. That was enough observing for me. I grabbed her slim waist and pushed her up. Her mouth opened as I exploded deep inside of her.

When it was over she put her hands on my shoulders and kissed me—a real kiss—a "thank you" from a woman. That was the only kiss we had shared. We lay there for awhile. Young that I was, a half an hour later I was ready for more, but she would have none of it. She quickly dressed, scarf included, glanced at me and headed down the trail.

There was something overtly disturbing about it all. How could she make love to me and remain so aloof? But it was more than that. The encounter seemed to have a ritualistic cloak wrapped around it.

I bundled together my clothing and went down to bathe in the pond below. The water was icy-cold, but I held my head under until it began to hurt from the numbness. Laying on a warm rock afterwards, wet and naked, I felt a cool tingling all over my body, like an electric current. Closing my eyes, it seemed that my body was surrounded by an indigo blue neon light that omitted tiny, slow flashes of powerful white elongated sparks. Even though I had sensed it from the first time I had drank some of the water high up on that frozen mountain, this was the first tangible experience that indicated there was something special about it, and this place. Since then, I have endeavored to re-create that experience. No matter how cold the water, or how calm and peaceful I have felt, all I have received is the slow flashes of the little fairy lights, and an occasional wink of the electric blue energy.

I remained at the pond for awhile and contemplated. Much of her sorrow, her pain, her loneliness, and her self-imposed penitence had been released along with her primal physical needs. Years later, a much wiser experienced man knew that Céline's release of energy that day was perfectly natural and healthy, and that my uncanny suspicions concerning the ritualistic aspect of the encounter were also accurate.

My weapon felt out of place in my hand as I left the area of the sacred spring and went down the path. I was in no hurry, and stopped twice to admire the beauty of the place: once to gaze out into the valley as the summer heat waves rose amongst the deciduous trees that swayed in the wind, their leaves flickering from gray to green, and again to observe a group of tiny birds taking turns bathing in the shallows of the stream on the edge of a mossy glen.

When I walked through the back gate, Xavier was taking his evening repose in the shade at the outdoor table. We drank his wine while he smoked his pipe.

Camille and Céline were in the kitchen preparing the meal.

Eventually I asked Xavier about the Prieuré de Sion. Even though it was difficult for me to understand him at times, he indicated that it was a noble secret society that had been working behind the scenes for centuries for the benefit of mankind. That is as much as he was willing to share, except that certain members were also involved in the French resistance. He held his forefinger to his lips for a moment in the sign of secrecy. I understood, and immediately remembered the photograph of their son Jacques on the China cabinet. The French resistance had been a successful, persistent thorn in the side of the German occupation since the fall of Paris in 1940.

Dinner that evening was a more subdued affair than the night before. Camille did what she needed to do, but seemed distracted, perhaps due to the processing of her dream and also her suspicions about what had occurred between Céline and I that afternoon.

Céline avoided eye contact with me, but was not unfriendly. She was certainly more relaxed, and drank enough wine to actually get a little tipsy.

Xavier reacted to the mood by being fussy about his food—requesting a little more of this and that. It was an annoying childlike reaction, especially since the meal was superb. Camille had Céline gather a few wild greens. She ground them together with some spinach and herbs from the garden, and with dried mushrooms and strong cheese had produced a delicious quiche. The quiche had been proceeded by fresh bread and onion soup in chicken broth. I certainly did not complain—Mr. eat Spam-out-of-a-can.

7

A Private War

The next morning it was time for me to take my leave. I delayed getting out of the comfortable, clean bed for awhile. It was next to a tall, narrow window that looked out over the little hamlet and further into the vineyards and fields below. Jacques's bedroom was next to Céline's; that mysterious woman who had captured my imagination and unwillingly the borderlands of my heart.

Our encounter the day before at the sacred spring was both exciting and disturbing. I suspected that Céline was genuinely attracted to me as I was to her—in spite of herself. She had already spent enough time mired in the dungeons of her sorrow and pain.

As I lay there quietly thinking about it, a steely kind of resolve began to form in my mind. If I can, and if she is willing, I will return to this place and make a family here. Perhaps I could even bring my mother here. The gentle lady would love this place, these people. She was like a fish out of water in rural Seattle.

When I went downstairs Camille was puttering around

in the kitchen. She had prepared a breakfast as well as a travel package of food for me. Xavier was already in the vineyard, and Céline had disappeared early, perhaps up to the spring.

I ate the breakfast, chatted with Camille, and studied the map on the wall of the local villages and roads. She showed me how I could skirt the roads and towns, and pointed out the major highway where the German forces were known to be still moving along. It wasn't far.

When I was ready to go, Céline still had not returned, but I could not linger there.

"I will say goodbye to Céline for you, Marc."

"Thank you. You have been generous, welcoming a common dirt soldier into your home."

"Somehow I think you are much more than that Marc. Besides, our thanks is to you for bringing the wild horse back to her stable."

"So I am a knight in shining armor; but the damsel in distress turns out to be ambivalent." I was probing.

She laughed at that. "I wouldn't be so sure. She has a fairies heart—fierce and delicate."

"I will return after the war is over."

"You do that Marc. Au revoir."

I understood. It was not wise to make too much of an emotional investment in a departing soldier heading towards the battle lines.

I stepped out the front door onto the cobbled street. Standing in the doorway, she called out after me, "Marc—be careful!"

She was investing more than she had intended.

I smiled, blew her a kiss and walked through the middle of the village, and out into the French countryside.

I found the trail Camille had told me about that went through the fields and wound down towards the highway. The late morning sun was warm as I passed through the shady woods, fields of grass and wildflowers with cows lazily munching on huge mouthfuls of it all.

How could there be war in a place such as this? And why? But war there was, which became apparent when I began to hear the telltale sound of urgent engines moving men and equipment on the highway below.

I found a little hollow under an oak tree, well above the road, with a good sized creek nearby. I was determined to wait there until American forces showed up. It had to be soon. German convoys of trucks, artillery, tanks and equipment were moving up the road in one direction only—north towards Germany. The trucks were filled with dirty, exhausted men. Men that were loosing the war. Men that were retreating towards their homes. Men that had killed many of my comrades-in-arms.

I felt mostly pity for them. War was insanity. I could not understand the point of it all. I had plenty of time to observe and contemplate up there. Almost two weeks passed before I saw any allied troops.

After two days hunger and boredom forced me to follow the bellowing sound of cows to a farmhouse nearby. I selected a small denomination bill and had it in hand as I knocked on the door. A woman opened it, and was obviously frightened by having a soldier on her front porch. I stepped back and spoke quickly. Camille had taught me how to properly ask for food, but I introduced myself first.

"Je m'appelle Marc—American."

"American?"

"Oui Madame."

The entire act had been planned and well rehearsed while I relaxed in my little hollow under the oak tree. I had my weapon slung over my shoulder, not in front of me, and the money in my hand.

She took the money, shut the door, and came back with a half a loaf of bread, some cheese, and a big mug of fresh milk. She handed me the milk first and told me to drink up. Perhaps it was merely due to my perpetual hunger, but I thought it was the best milk I had ever had, with a lot of cream. I told her so. She pointed to the cows nearby, and shrugged proudly while I handed the mug back. I thanked her twice and left.

Two days later when I went for a repeat performance the dairyman himself was there. He was not afraid of me, but wanted to know why I was in the area. At that point my limited French language skills failed me, so after lifting up a thick finger, and telling me to wait, he brought out a small, old leather bound French/English dictionary.

"I am waiting for the Americans to arrive."

He understood that, but wanted to know how I had gotten there.

"Parachute" was a word not included in that dictionary, being a new invention in those days. I asked for paper and a pencil, drew a picture of a parachute with a man hanging beneath it, pointed to the man, said "Moi," and showed him the airborne wing insignia on my jacket.

He was impressed. In those days, simply the notion of someone willingly leaping from an airplane with only a skimpy silk parachute lent one a kind of automatic heroic status.

The farmer was curious about my trousers, so I told him they were a gift from Monsieur Xavier Favreau. They knew the Favreau family. Apparently they attended mass at the same church. I should have known. The Favreau family owned much of the land in the village nearby.

Two days later the German traffic had slowed considerably. Only two vehicles had passed by in the morning. Later in the day a thunderstorm rolled in, the grey clouds interrupting the patchy sunshine. By the time I made it to the farmhouse it was raining heavily. This time they invited me in to eat with them.

They were a middle-aged couple, with photographs of their children and grandchildren on the bureau. It was simple fare: beef soup, bread, cheese, milk, and wine—and plenty of it. She had made all of the food from scratch.

After dinner, they told me that they had spoken with Madame Favreau after mass earlier that morning (I didn't even know that it was Sunday). My hostess made a dramatic point to inform me that Madame Céline had given me her regards. The stocky farm wife stood there with a hand upside down on a hip grinning at me until I raised my hand and feigned to fan myself because of the heat. She laughed and laughed. It seemed, at least according to the peasants, that I was now a legitimate contender for the throne.

They let me sleep in the barn. There was no way that I would sleep in that house. There was no cover around it for me to escape if it was deemed necessary. The barn backed up against the woods, and I was comfortable in there on the dry hay with the sound of the rain pelting down on the roof.

It was still drizzling in the morning, so I helped the farmer shovel some hay and manure. As I was watching him milk the cows, we heard the sound of a truck coming up the drive. I knew the signature tone of those engines well, having listened to them for over a week. I grabbed my gear and ducked out the back, moving fast out and around through the trees, flanking the German truck, and took up a position eighty yards down the drive behind a big rock.

There were three of them, an officer and two soldiers. The dairyman and his wife were both in front of the house. I could hear the officer aggressively speaking in French to the farmer, who kept shaking his head sideways. The officer pulled out his pistol, held it to the woman's head, and yelled at the dairyman.

I realized that I did not even know the names of this simple couple that had been so kind to me. The sight of the soldiers mortally threatening the innocent woman was so appalling that it stirred up the rumblings of a protective predatory instinct in me. If they had merely asked for food and been on their way I would have allowed them to pass—but not now. *This was war.* Those three men had already seen their last sunrise.

The farmer went into the house and brought out a small strongbox. He stubbornly stood there holding it, until one of the soldiers stepped over and grabbed it from his hands. The two soldiers got in the truck and turned it around. The officer still had his weapon pointed at the woman's head. Finally, he backed up with it still trained on them until he stepped into the passenger seat.

It was a robbery, plain and simple—a cruel routine they had performed before.

What followed was more akin to an assassination than battle. I was a few feet above the road, and very close to it. I melted into the rock. When the truck got to my position it was still going through the gears and moving slowly. I aimed, and waited until all three of their heads were lined up like dominoes. The lieutenant saw me right before I opened fire.

Too bad—Welcome to hell.

The bullets went in through the open side window and out the open drivers side window, taking a hat, a helmet, and much of the material from the soldiers' heads with them. It was an ugly, gory scene.

The woman was still standing in the same place, sobbing. The dairyman moved towards me as I stepped around and pulled the bodies out, grabbed the strongbox and handed it to him. He didn't say anything. He just stood there looking at me with the box in his hands. Finally he turned, walked towards the house, put an arm around his wife and led her inside.

The jackals' pockets were stuffed with money and jewelry. After awhile the farmer came out. We got rid of the bodies with his hay wagon.

I tried to convince him to keep the truck. At first it was a flat-out no. It was a filthy German thing. I saw it as a really fine piece of equipment that could be an asset to his farm. I pantomimed painting it in blue, red and white French colors. We had to do something with it, and the German army was almost gone. Pride versus practicality. He didn't agree to anything, but we threw buckets of water on the seat and the dashboard and parked it out in his back pasture, hidden by some trees.

That evening, even though I apologized repeatedly for what had happened, they insisted that I join them for dinner. When the meal was prepared we prayed.

I am generally not religious in any orthodox fashion, but that night I prayed: I prayed for those beautiful, simple people that had sheltered me. I prayed for the German soldiers I had killed. I hadn't really sent them to hell. I didn't believe in it. They had created their own hell. I prayed for all of the French people. I prayed for all of the German people. I really had no grudge against them. I prayed for all the people of our world; may we never have another world war. I prayed for Céline.

When the dairyman and his wife were not looking I slipped a big wad of bills in their bureau drawer. I slept in the hay and got up even before they did.

That day I saw two Sherman tanks rumbling up the highway followed by a few soldiers. The tanks looked small compared to the German Panzers I'd seen earlier.

Later in the day a contingent of Marines arrived on foot. They were battle-worn veterans.

The Marine Captain sized me up. He had the brown-stained stub of what remained of a burnt-out cigarette stuck to the side his lower lip. As he talked the thing moved up and down. "I know you airborne guys think you're tough, but I can't take an Army grunt with us. We're Marines. We speak a different language."

The guys chuckled. They looked like regular American soldiers to me, chewing gum and smoking cigarettes.

I must have presented an unusual picture, with the trousers and the glossy black German pistol belt.

"It looks like you've been having your own private little war up here anyway corporal."

They moved on without me.

The next morning, three trucks came up the road filled with Australian soldiers. Their attitude was quite different. "Sure, hop on mate."

They were cocky and funny. We ended up drinking wine and rambunctiously swimming in the Rhône river.

The next day they dumped me off with a hangover at a US Army field base. I presented myself to the Major in command. He was really too busy for me, which was to become the theme for almost every encounter I had with the "brass" for the remaining time I spent in France. In no way could the needs of one lost soldier be put high on any priority list. I summarized my story and showed the Major the orders I had found on the SS officer.

He glanced at the paper, and looked at the little SS pin, "Nice souvenir. Is that the officer's pistol?"

I demurred.

"Don't worry corporal, I won't take your weapon. But would you mind if I take a look at it?"

I handed him the pistol.

He examined it closely. "A Walther PP. I've heard about these. Nice piece." He handed it back.

"As much as I need every good man I can get out here on the front, I have to send you back to headquarters in Paris. You've got to report to the spooks."

"Spooks?"

"Spies corporal. Anything to do with the SS they want to handle. Ever heard of the OSS?"

"Yes sir, we had two OSS officers on our jump three weeks ago into the Jura mountains."

"Yup, you're going to Paris then. You can hitch a ride on one of those supply trucks parked out there."

An hour later, orders in hand I was on my way to Paris. Once there, I presented myself at headquarters. It was a place bustling with activity. I was eventually ushered in to the clean, orderly office of a Captain.

"You're out of uniform soldier."

I stammered an excuse.

"Get a new set of trousers at the PX pronto. And what's that weapon you are carrying?"

"A German pistol sir."

"That's not authorized ordinance corporal."

Pencil pusher

After showing him my orders, he told me where to find the OSS office.

It took all day, but when I was finally ushered into the office of an OSS Major, I handed him my orders.

"So you took out an SS Standartenführer? Good job corporal."

He looked at the holster. "Walther PP?"

"Yes sir."

"Nice souvenir."

I handed him the SS officer's orders. He studied them for awhile. "Was he carrying any documents?

"Documents?"

"Yes, didn't you check him for documents?"

"I was a soldier in the field sir. When I shoot someone I generally don't think about documents."

"You searched him and retrieved these orders."

"Yes sir, but I didn't find any other documents."

He studied me for a few moments.

I had been dutifully following what I thought was the correct course of action—to report what I had found to my superiors.

Why was I doing this? Why didn't I just keep it all to myself?

"Tell me about the SS officer. How did you kill him?"

It felt like the Inquisition. I related the story almost as it happened, omitting Céline's presence, and the strongbox. It was a reasonably believable story.

"But then you searched their bodies."

"Yes sir."

"Why did you do that?"

"I was hungry."

"Did you take their money?"

"Yes sir, and I bought food with it."

"From whom?"

"I would knock on the doors of farmhouses and hold out one of the bills. The locals helped me."

He had reservations, but he had to accept it.

This officer had never been a dirt soldier.

"Sir, do you know what happened to the other soldiers in my unit?"

"That information is classified corporal."

They were my comrades—not his.

After I left his office, I vowed to never willingly put myself in that position again. I wised up, and stayed in Paris for four months; making myself as scarce as possible without being declared AWOL.

No one cared. Paris was great. I had plenty of money; visited the Louvre, museums, archaeological sites, and spent time in cafés.

Towards the end of my tenure there, I received notification from the army that my mother had died in an auto accident. The war was almost over.

They sent me home.

8

French Angels

The passing of my mother was difficult for me in ways that I choose not to dwell on here.

The day I arrived I knelt down in the flower garden and thought about her. It didn't matter that it was late winter. The flowers were not blooming, but this was the place that she loved. This was the only refuge where she would hum to herself as she was pruning, weeding or gathering flowers. The lady of grace asked for so little. The only things I kept of hers were the photographs, her jewelry, and the tea set.

It took another six months to fulfill my duties with the US armed forces. When I tried to sell the house on Three Tree Point to finance my return to France, I found out that it had not actually been owned by her. It was held in a trust. I hired a local attorney to sort it out, but he didn't understand it either. It was a trust within a trust within a trust; all incorporated on the Isle of Man off of the coast of England.

I gave up, rented the house and went back to work for the Boeing aircraft company.

I finally managed to return to France in the spring of 1947.

I had written numerous letters to Madame Favreau, but received only two in return. I took the train to New York, a ship to England, another boat to France and a train to Paris. In Paris I bought a cheap car and drove out towards Savoie.

The old cottage looked exactly as it did the last time I saw it, with the open sardine tin still on the table. The strongbox was safe where I had hidden it, buried behind a rock too large to be moved by a machine.

The Mercedes staff car was still there. I put a new battery in it, started it up and let it run while I cleaned it up, then painted the whole car with a can of dark blue paint.

The following day I drove to the Swiss border. The taciturn border guards let me through after being told I was on banking business.

Knowing nothing about Swiss banks, I walked in to the first one I saw. It was certainly not the biggest, but it turned out to be the oldest bank in Geneva.

The Swiss English-speaking banker they assigned to me was businesslike and reserved. He took one of the coins and spun it on the marble counter top.

"Is that some sort of arcane ritual for a new customer?"

That got a chuckle out of him.

"This is how we determine if the coin is real. These French angels are obviously genuine, but I must perform the—'ritual' anyway."

He had a sense of humor after all.

"I am listening to the sound of the coin. Pure gold has an unmistakably clear, beautiful tone. A false coin made of base metal that has been plated rings quite differently." He held up a well manicured finger. "I will show you."

He opened a drawer, brought out a shiny gold coin and spun it on the marble.

"Can you hear the difference?"

"Yes, the plated coin sounds harsh and tinny."

"Excellent descriptive. Tin, as well as Zinc are easily cast-able metals often used by counterfeiters."

He then proceeded to methodically set up an account for me.

The next day I returned with the bulk of the coins. It was a bold move, and I was nervous with all of it in the car. The bank had an organized routine for processing bullion. I parked in a special place, and guards unloaded the strongbox onto a metal cart and rolled it into the bank. It was counted and carefully weighed; all supervised by the banker and myself.

He talked me into allowing the bank to invest some of the funds for me. He showed me a list of companies they were investing in at the time. Many were American; Boeing being one.

"Yes, we are recommending investing heavily in some American companies at this time. The U.S.A. may be in a temporary recession now, but that will not last long. It's all historically predictable."

"What do you mean?"

He moved forward in his chair. I could tell he had a passion for this. "Think about it. The war is over, and virtually all of the economies and infrastructures of the free industrialized nations in the world are in shambles.

Except one. Germany has been beaten into the ground. France is struggling to rebuild. Italy is in a perpetual state of disorganization. During the war, much of the residual wealth from Great Britain ended up in the bank accounts of American companies and factory workers. England paid heavily for its freedom. American factories that were built during the war are state of the art, with skilled workers and supplied by a seemingly unlimited amount of raw materials. Factor in the typical American ingenuity and what we will see are high quality products marketed at reasonable prices for the next several decades; with virtually no competition! I predict that in twenty years there will be an affluent middle class in America."

He continued, "Because of the temporary recession in the U.S.A., stocks are inexpensive now. It is an excellent time to buy. We are investing primarily in industry, heavy industry and agriculture."

"You really know what you're talking about don't you?"

"I did graduate from a business school in London specializing in high finance."

I let him put one half of the gold into investments. It was a very wise move.

9

Gentleman Nouveau

I went shopping in Geneva. I bought a blue dress for Céline, a tea set for Camille and a French Calabash pipe for Xavier. For myself I purchased new clothing, shoes and a wristwatch. The selection of watches was overwhelming, so I chose one that I liked the look of: a Patek Phillipe automatic with Roman numerals in a solid gold case with a cognac-colored crocodile leather band. It was a gorgeous thing. For the first time in my life I paid no attention to the prices.

The shopping was fun. My plan had worked. I had triumphed, and was now a man of means. However, when I emerged from watch shop I realized how tired I was. An insisting exhaustion settled down over me, and began to envelope my senses in a clear, thick cloud of numbness. Looking back, it must have been the culmination of an entire chapter of the saga; beginning when I had jumped out into that moonless night sky over the Jura mountains three years earlier.

I woke up on top of a bed immobilized, not knowing where I was, and for a moment, who I was. It was one of those afternoon naps where you go in so deep that you are completely disoriented when you wake up.

I was in Geneva in a hotel room. The last bits of amber light from the sun highlighted the ornate Gothic creatures on the upper façade of the building across the street. My mind was free for the moment, so I studied them for awhile, pondering why they would choose such grotesque images for decorations.

My stomach cried out to me, insisting. I stumbled down the stairs and into a restaurant around the corner. The tables were full, so I stepped up to the bar. There was a gentleman sitting there that I recognized. I knew no one in Geneva. He looked back at me.

Still groggy, I said it in English, "Where do I know you from?"

"Monsieur Rémillard?" It was not really a question.

It was the banker.

I stammered, "Oh, I'm sorry. I just woke up from a nap."

"Quite alright. Please, sit down and have a drink. But I should tell you that we cannot discuss bank business here."

"I wouldn't think of it."

He held out his hand. "Raoul."

"Marc."

Of all the people in the world, this was the only man who suspected that I had just gone from rags to riches.

"Did you buy that watch today?"

"Yes, I know very little about quality watches. I just liked the style of it."

"May I see it?" He was a watch aficionado. He quickly looked at it and handed it back, "Good choice—really! It may be attractive, but it also has a very good movement—and made here in Geneva."

We talked for a while until a table became available. He invited me to join him. We had dinner together, along with two bottles of wine.

Raoul had a great mind, with a focus on international economics and politics. He read profusely, and was aware of events developing in many countries. We eventually ended up talking about women. He liked women, which was obvious by the way his eyes followed our waitress.

"I have been trying to get her to go out with me for six months, but she has a boyfriend."

He had numerous short-lived relationships, but the more he talked the more obvious it became why he was still single. He was eccentrically picky. The correct woman for him was out there somewhere, but to qualify, her characteristic traits had to first match his carefully chosen set of criteria. It was a long list, some of which made no rational sense at all. An example being that he was a devout Catholic, but didn't care if she was or not. He actually preferred if she wasn't. I was certainly no expert on women, but listened wryly.

Raoul didn't like German women because they were too bossy, Swiss women because they were cold, or French ladies because of inborn pride and haughtiness. He liked Italian women.

I chided him, "Perhaps you should move to Italy Raoul?"

"I don't have to. I can go there and get one any time I like!"

He didn't drive.

"Well I don't see one sitting here with us."

He shrugged his shoulders.

"Listen—aren't you limiting your playing field just a little by dismissing entire nations of the fairer sex? Out of millions of German women there must be several that are not domineering. In all of France, there is certainly at least one demure, placid lady. I'll bet there are Swiss girls that are wild and vivacious."

"There are no Swiss women like that."

It was an absolute. A law of Physics.

We laughed and laughed. It was a good time.

Towards the end of the evening a thought came to me. "Do you know what the Prieuré de Sion is?"

"One of the many secret societies in Europe with delusions of grandeur. It's kind of a wealthy gentleman's club that is obsessed with the notion of being old French royalty."

"I thought that ended with the French revolution."

"Yes and no. They believe that their heritage goes back much further. It has something to do with Jesus and Mary Magdalene having children, and spawning the Merovingian Dynasty."

"When was that?"

"During the Dark Ages. The church strongly considers the idea heretical. The Prieuré de Sion are a very secretive group. The only reason I know about them is because my brother is a Swiss Guard."

"Swiss Guard?"

"A special contingent of soldiers that guard the Pope."

"Oh yes, I've heard of them, but why would he know about the Prieuré de Sion?"

"Its his business to protect the Vatican from heretical fanatics, and once in a while there are some problems with them. He is not supposed to tell me about his work. Perhaps you shouldn't mention it to anyone."

With that, the evening ended, but I knew exactly where to find Raoul when I found myself in Geneva.

It turned out that his habits were regular and predictable, like the Swiss watches that were manufactured in the neighborhood. Every morning he ate at the same cafe, and every evening at 6:00 he had a drink at one of two restaurants, followed by dinner at a table. On Sundays he would attend mass with his mother, followed by an afternoon meal prepared by her. He didn't cook—it was far too messy. As worldly as Raoul was, most of his life was spent within a radius of a few blocks.

Men need drinking buddies. Visiting Geneva to withdraw funds from the bank became a regular occurrence in the year that followed. Sometimes after dinner Raoul and I would walk down the street and knock on the door of one of his friends, a small fair-skinned Italian named Davide, who worked at one of the watch factories. It was the same routine every time: Davide would answer the door, then look back down the hallway as if in fear of someone, grab his coat and slip out the door, closing it quietly. We would then proceed to a nearby pub, where we would imbibe in lager beers until our heads were pounding.

10

Test of Fire

The next morning I drove back to the l'ermitage ancienne. That is what they called it; that little stone cottage with the leaky roof that an American paratrooper once used as a refuge in August of 1944. From the brief time I had spent with the Favreau family three years earlier, I gathered that the place was intended to serve as a retreat; a haven for contemplation and meditation for those spiritually focused enough to find it. There was no lock on the door, and it featured the austerity of a monks cell. In all the time I spent there, I was never aware of anyone else visiting the place. I don't know what a hermit looks like, and I'm not sure whether I'd recognize one if I saw him, or her. Perhaps *I'm* the hermit, as I seem to be the only soul who frequents the place.

When I pulled in that late morning I realized there was no reason for me to go there. I turned the engine off and sat in the car for awhile.

It was time to go to Céline, but I hesitated. I feared being turned away.

It was more frightening than jumping out of an airplane, tougher than soldiering, and harder than laboring. All of the hope, desire, emotions, thoughts and preparations had coalesced into a loose bundle that I unwillingly carried; like that old parachute—but much heavier. Our thought forms may be burdensome at times, but they are in fact how we create our reality—for better or for worse. The inevitable struggle with ourselves and the outside world is like the grist in a mill; necessary to grind the flour of our souls finer. But the mill also produces heat, a fire within, rendering us more powerful. If we could only approach each day fresh, like a child, we would indeed be much happier. In fact, the massive weight of the past is the bane of the elderly. Perhaps that is why we age after all. I thought about those things while I sat there.

I turned the key in the dashboard of the Mercedes, and eight minutes later was parked in front of the house.

The door opened almost immediately after I engaged the knocker. Xavier had just come in from the vineyards and was taking his boots off in the entry. He didn't recognize me and was very formal, "Bonjour, may I help you?"

"Monsieur Favreau...I am Marc Rémillard, American soldier?" It took a long moment for it to register. He suddenly transformed into the warm, animated Xavier. "Marc, of course, come in, come in." He grabbed me by the shoulders affectionately and kissed me on both cheeks in the manner of French men of the older generation. It was odd feeling a man's bristles on my face.

"Camille, see who has come to visit—the most beautiful of men. Marc, look at you." He flared his hands out and tilted his head in another very Gaulish gesture.

I must have looked rather dapper in my new Swiss clothing.

Madame Favreau stepped into the room. She was the epitome of the French lady: elegant, gracious, worldly, reserved but friendly, both formal and informal, practical but passionately impractical—all rolled up into an attractive package.

I was in a state of raw emotional openness.

"Bonjour Marc," she said.

"Bonjour Madame."

Céline appeared in the doorway. She was in a light green dress sporting an apron with baking flour on it. A child materialized—a little girl clinging on to her leg. *Her child.*

The color must have drained from my face.

Madame Favreau took command of the situation, asked Céline to make us some tea, and led me through the dining room and out onto the back veranda.

The little birds fled in a flurry. I could hear the sound of the stream as it fell from the stone fountain. The maple leaves fluttered in the breath of the warm, dry sirocco wind, which had found a final resting place there at the foot of the Jura mountains after blowing in over the Mediterranean sea from the Sahara desert.

She spoke in English. "Marc, it is good to see you. How have you been?"

"Quite well, thank you. Did you receive my letters?"

"Yes, and I am glad you have come to visit us, but I admit to being confused about your intentions."

Her stark frankness could be considered by some to be impolite, but I didn't see it that way. Her bold honesty was one of the things I liked about her.

She had the innate ability to slice right to the heart of the matter. It was in fact, a matter of the heart. She was looking up at me, studying me with those keen, blue perceptive eyes.

It was a time for truth, but I stammered. "Well... I thought that perhaps...you know I do not have a family. I thought maybe I could make a family here."

She waited. Why is it so difficult for men to express that which is so dear to them? A genetic defect perhaps? It is a psychological enigma. Men, who bluster so boldly. Men, who go to war, toil, and struggle with adversities foreign to the female consciousness. Perhaps a man's heart is even more fragile than a woman's. Perhaps not. It is certainly more guarded.

I finally spat it out. "I came for Céline, but I had not considered that she may have already married."

She grabbed my arm and gave it a little shake. It was a friendly—*snap out of it you dullard* gesture.

"Marc...The child is yours."

My jaw dropped. She produced a triumphal little smirk. I looked over at the girl playing on the table through the window. Camille still hadn't released her hold on my arm. The woman was relentless. She was testing me, and was not done with me yet. Madame Favreau was a wolverine protecting her brood.

"What would you do with a child such as that?"

"What do you mean?"

"What kind of a father would you be?"

I understood. "I would treat her like an angel, of course!" I meant it.

That is what she wanted to hear, but continued to stare into my face for a long moment.

The wolverine finally let go of my arm, stepped back and lit up a cigarette; giving me time to digest it all.

I kept staring at the child through the window. The girl looked up at me, smiled and waved.

I began to feel a subtle warmth flow into me. It started at the very tips of my toes and progressed slowly through the rest of my body. It was a fabric of fluid energy that I had not missed or been aware of, but that I somehow remembered.

It was one of those rare potent experiences that become pivotal moments in our lives, acquiring ever more luster as time passes. Some memories remain forever in our consciousness, branded upon our minds in the moment of their creation without intention on our part. I will never forget when I first feasted my eyes on my daughter.

I have always had the innate ability to recognize a historical event as it is occurring. Somehow, I can observe a situation as one would see it decades, or even hundreds of years in the future. During those moments of rarefied objectivity I have felt very old and wise—much older than a normal human lifespan.

When the supple flow of warmth reached my head it became so overwhelming that I began to tear-up. They were simple tiny tears. It had been three long years since I had met Céline—and like an avalanche, much of the hope, expectations, and stress of my mothers passing tumbled out at that one moment.

Camille had been watching me, not as the wolverine but as a family member—curious, compassionate and interested. I allowed her to see it.

"You know Marc, I liked you the first time I saw you. You have a child-like purity of spirit about you."

She took another puff.

"You should also know that you have become somewhat of a legend in the villages around here."

She held the cigarette expressively, like a paint brush or a baton. "The American who descended from the sky. He whose feet graced the very tip of the mountain, followed the sacred spring down through the meadows, dispatched two powerful Nazi officers to hell where they belong, only to complete his brief sojourn amongst us by impregnating the lovely priestess."

The lady had a sardonic wit and a keen sense of drama. She raised her eyebrows. "Not to mention spattering the brains of three German thieves all over Monsieur and Madame Theury's drive!"

I had been naughty and was being scolded by my favorite aunt. I picked up the thread and capitulated.

"Yes, that was kind of messy—in rather bad taste I admit."

"Somehow afterwards, God chose to grace the couple with a cash stipend for their suffering!"

"Really!" I feigned ignorance.

Her eyes narrowed. "The only glimpse the villagers had of you is when you walked out of town three years ago. They dote over Monique as if she were a star-child."

She paused for a moment and reflected. "Perhaps she is. Our young benevolent local priest is of course very uncomfortable with all of it.

She raised her eyebrows and cocked her head to press a point. "Consider going very slowly with Céline. She is strong but delicate. She's somewhat of a thoroughbred."

I took Madame Favreau's advise very seriously, and treated Céline gently. I did not even try to touch her at first. My insecure fears that she would have to be convinced, courted, or not welcome my affections were completely unjustified. It became immediately apparent that she *wanted* me to be there with her. It was both a breath of fresh air as well as a deep watering in my garden patch of stunted, withering plants.

My command of the French language had improved enough for us to actually get to know one another. Céline had a quick mind and a lyrical sense of humor. I genuinely liked her. She responded in kind. She had been lonely, as I had.

What sealed it was my interactions with our daughter Monique—which was easy. Three-year-old children are intrinsically charming creatures anyway, and this one just happened to bear a strong resemblance to me.

The third day I decided to give the women a break from my presence in and around the house, so I went to work with Xavier in the vineyards. We spent the day thinning the extra shoots from the growing grapevines. It's one of those jobs that some may deem boring and tedious, while others find to be relaxing. I enjoyed it. Xavier showed me how to thin the excessive growth, and tie up the functional growing shoots, exposing the grape clusters to the sun. He claimed that it would encourage the vines to ripen the grapes better.

We worked back to back as he taught me the task at hand. He was more than happy to have my help, but also wanted to ensure that I didn't butcher any of his beloved grapevines.

That day I began to realize how good of a vigneron Xavier was. He was an artist. His knowledge of the vines and grapes went deep into the intuitive realm. Xavier was able to coax his vines to produce good enough grapes to make decent wine at an altitude higher than they should be growing. His vineyards averaged about 400 meters above sea level. They were planted in the Altesse white grape variety; a local rarity. They yielded a very crisp, dry, drinkable wine.

We had plenty of time to talk that day. I still had difficulty understanding much of Xavier's French, particularly when he became animated and began to speak rapidly. One particular conversation I found interesting, but I had to question him about it until I understood.

Xavier claimed that what causes some rare vineyards in the world to consistently yield great wines is due to their unique geographical locations. He said that only a few vineyards are fortunate enough to have what he termed "noblesse", which is the melding of two distinct factors: "noble", and "bless".

If a vineyard was situated on a "noble" site, that would mean that it was a physically ideal place for a particular grape variety to grow. The soil types, sub-soil types, elevation, latitude, orientation to the sun, and steepness of the slope all come into play. The term "terroir" is used in France commonly to describe the overall physical characteristics of a grape growing location.

The other factor Xavier claimed to be synonymous with great vineyards was the "bless" element, which was far less known, accepted or understood by vignerons worldwide than the concept of terroir. According to Xavier, this was sacred knowledge that filtered down from the ancient mystery schools, the Prieuré de Sion, the Rosicrucians, and other secret orders.

Xavier explained how the Earth had electro-magnetic

lines of force, or *ley* lines that circled it much like our hypothetical longitude and latitude lines. Birds used the longitudinal oriented ley lines as navigational guides when they migrate between northern and southern locations. Wherever the longitudinal and latitudinal lines cross, they merge at that point into a power spot. There is therefore, an abundance of electro-magnetic energy at power spots.

In Europe, many of those places have been the sites for shrines for thousands of years, and are considered sacred places by the local populace. Many Catholic churches have been built atop older Visigoth shrines, which were in turn Celtic shrines before them. The great cathedrals of France were purposefully built on the intersections of ley lines.

If a vineyard happens to be on or near a power spot it is "blessed". Plants grow healthier there . They are simply biological creatures responding to the enhanced energy.

Xavier explained that his vineyards did not have ideal terroir. The soil and slopes were good, but they were situated at too high of an elevation. His vineyards did not have the "noble" part of noblesse.

There was however, an intersection of ley lines nearby at the sacred spring. That is why there is an ancient Celtic shrine there. The stream that flows down the mountain into the Favreaus' back yard follows the course of a ley line.

"You Marc, like a bird migrating from east to west followed the ley line down the mountain to become part of our family—the caretakers of the spring. Have you ever noticed how nourishing the water is? I am a good vigneron, but this vineyard is blessed. That is why I can ask higher prices for the wine."

Therefore, the next day, when Céline asked me if I wanted to have a picnic at the sacred spring, I saw it from a quite different perspective.

Camille offered to look after Monique, and gave us a bottle of her fine red Musigny to take with us, which was essentially endorsing us 120 percent.

Céline wore the blue summer dress I had bought in Geneva for her, and brought a blanket. I carried the basket with the food and wine.

We were excited and happy to be together. We talked, ate, drank water, enjoyed the wine and made love.

I began to tune in to that place. There is a certain timelessness about it that is difficult to define. Before long the sun was going down. We had been there since noon but it felt like only several hours had passed. I questioned Céline about it. She was much more reserved than Xavier had been.

Kneeling on her heels—her dark, fine, lustrous hair tousled and falling over her shoulders, she contemplated for a moment. "Some of the physicists claim that time may actually be spherical in nature, not linear, as we tend to assume." She paused to think again before explaining further. "Time is a creation of men based on the movement of the planets in an effort to normalize our place in the cosmos, but it is not an absolute as many think. What about our dream time? It follows no such rules. Perhaps this place ticks more to the clock of dream time—no?"

She counseled me to be patient.

11

The Wedding

We were married in the little Catholic church in the nearby village. The absurd medieval restrictions imposed upon widows by the church tends to be ignored during and after wars; particularly concerning local celebrities, both famous and infamous.

Popularity is an amazing phenomenon. It can capture the imagination and focus of a population, and with little effort, hurtles over social barriers, nullifies belief systems, and transcends class distinctions. As fleeting and temporal as it was, for a brief time in that quaint corner of France—Céline and I were the talk of the town.

We were to be married. The young Father Bouchet was compelled to do a predictable dance concerning the issue, but in the end he had to relent. He really had no choice. The ceremony could either be performed by him or an official at the local government office. Better be that sinners are taken into the fold of the church rather than left to wander in the wilderness without spiritual guidance.

On the day of our wedding the weather was unusually balmy, with little knobby renaissance clouds perched in the sky high above. They looked like the clouds that I had seen in old paintings at the Louvre; clouds that appeared to have taken a considerable amount of effort to create. Perhaps the fickle gods of the *Iliad* were restlessly waiting to observe our humble affair—lingering on their puffy, classically-shaped marshmallows.

It was also a bit breezier that day than one would hope for a wedding reception, but it lent a kind of intangible flavor to the proceedings. I felt it was appropriate actually. It was our day, and it was as if we had chosen the weather to precisely reflect our attitude towards life. Nature was ancient—eons old, while their god was merely a young upstart—the new kid on the block. The fact that he had managed to bully his way into our wedding ceremony we begrudgingly accepted. It served to placate the community at large. Dovetailing with the local society was something the Favreau family had worked hard to maintain for reasons I did not begin to understand until later. *They were hiding.* That however, we shall elaborate on later.

As usual I woke up early, fed Monique, then left her in the company of the women. It was inappropriate for me to be in the house when they were preparing. That is one of the aspects of the wedding ceremony that seems to be universal irregardless of culture or religion: the bride and groom must be separated for a while.

Ritual is an interesting phenomenon—like a giant primordial language that affects the subconscious in the long term. Each part of a ritual is like one letter, or a character in a word. The words make up sentences, to form paragraphs, which eventually become a story, and finally a saga is created. We can sense the letters, but they are much too large for us to see—perhaps from the ground all the way up to the clouds where the gods are reclining and waiting. The style of each letter reflects or is created by the nature of the ritual and the individuals involved.

This particular ritual I respected. Before Céline arose, I bathed, gathered up my dress clothes, carefully put them in the front seat of my car, and drove up to the l'ermitage ancienne. There I sat on the stone bench looking out at the valley for a long time. Typically quite comfortable in my own presence, I wasn't lonely, not even lonesome— but I did feel alone and contemplative. I thought about my mother. It seemed unfair she could not be here now. I hoped somehow she was. Who really knows about the afterlife? We are all barred from knowing about it, no matter what anyone portends. No minister, no priest, no Buddhist monk—no religion knows. Scientists don't know. Wherever my mother is, I hope she is happy for me.

My mind cannot stay inactive for long. Inevitably designs and ideas begin to flow in. I found I had turned and was looking at the old hermitage building itself. For the first time I more carefully studied the details in it's design. It was definitely in need of a new roof; in fact, the timbers that supported the thatch were rotting. The entire roof structure needed replacing. Upon closer examination, I could tell that the rafters and purlins had been split and hewn by hand. The roof had been made prior to the invention of the sawmill. What the building really deserved was a restoration, not a renovation.

I had a practical idea. What if I bought over-sized

rough-cut lumber, and had it planed down by hand to make it look like it had been hand hewn? The boards could then be stained and grimed-up to make them appear old.

A good idea always gets me jazzed-up, so I decided to walk the kilometer down to the ruined chateau to survey that site. I had already asked Céline what she thought about us building a new house there. I felt that it was her decision, since she already had her own history wrapped up in the place. She was keen to the idea.

I had driven by the site many times, but I had not actually walked there since the morning I had coaxed Céline out of the cellar. Except for a greater population of weeds, the place was unchanged. I went into the coolness of the cellar. Nothing had been moved—a scene from the past. What was left of the colonel's candle was still stuck to the shelf, and rough pockmarks from my Tommy-gun bullets peppered the stone wall under it. It all seemed like so long ago at the time, but there it was; a piece of my fateful history undisturbed. I had thought about getting rid of it, but when I realized that the cellar, or *cave,* as they call them in France, was exactly that. It, as well as the stairs had been carved out of the solid limestone bedrock. It was too valuable and practical to fill in. I lit the candle and took it deeper into the cellar to examine the interior. In the back of the cave the floor dropped down a step, and the ceiling was taller. What appeared to be a cistern was carved out of the solid rock against the back wall. The top of it was higher than my head. Two more smaller cisterns were next to it; each one lower than the last one. There were holes in the sides of the bottoms which would allow water to flow from the larger cistern down into the adjacent smaller one, and in turn into the last one. Later, Xavier told me that the arrangement was actually a gravity-fed red wine fermenting system. The grapes were crushed by foot in the upper vat, and then after fermentation the wine would be allowed to flow into the smaller vat below for secondary fermentation, and finally into the lowest one for clarification before drinking or putting into a barrel or amphora. He said that no one knew how old it was, but it could date back to the Roman era when, for several hundred years the temperatures in the area were warmer and more red grapes were grown.

I went up and surveyed the limestone cliff behind the ruins. If they had, in the days of yore, carved a cellar out of solid rock, we should—with dynamite, jack-hammers, and modern equipment be able to hack away at the base of the cliff. That would enable the house to be situated further from the road. Standing there, I began to formulate some ideas. The beauty of the site was that it was pleasantly isolated, and it commanded a majestic territorial view. I gathered that Céline liked the place because of the earth-energy there. I never understood much of what was going on in her mind—and I still don't. She maintains one foot in the physical world and another elsewhere.

Presently it was time for me to go, so I made my way back up the road, where I donned my dress clothes in the cool, musty darkness of the l'ermitage ancienne.

As I waited in the heart of the church, I was more nervous than I had thought I would be, but aware that I was also picking up on the excitement of the crowd. Father Bouchet stood quietly behind me. Ours was to be his first wedding ceremony in the diocese.

Suddenly, an angel appeared on the other end of the aisle—a regal being dressed in white. She was so beautiful—otherworldly, that the audience stopped and stared—some with their mouths open. She had temporarily lifted one foot out of the physical world and placed it where her other one resided: in that realm of visions, dreams, and unseen energies. She was allowing us all a rare glimpse of the private part of herself; the world where she actually lived much of the time. An elven queen had chosen to grace us all with a rare visit. Unlike most blushing brides, Céline was composed, performing the ritual with a natural, flowing grace. The sheer impact of her appearance was so powerful that I felt unexpected little pockets of fear from the audience. I looked up at the stained-glass windows in the church. *Mother, I hope you can see this.*

She was accompanied by Xavier who, when he wasn't dressed in his tattered vineyard clothes could out-class anyone in the territory.

When she stepped up I noticed something odd and familiar about her dress, but couldn't place it. Partway through the ceremony I glanced over at Céline while Father Bouchet was mumbling something in Latin, and realized that there were exposed, heavy duty, triple-stitched seams running across the shoulders of her dress that lent it kind of a formal, pseudo-military look. They had used part of my old parachute in the design of the dress. In some odd kind of a way it was appropriate, and yet the absurdity of it struck me in my funny bone. *A wedding dress built for combat.* I had to stifle it, but Father Bouchet gave me a knowing smile—misplacing my emotion for another one entirely.

Later, at the reception, while dancing with Camille I brought the subject up.

"By the way, I like the design of the wedding dress," I commented.

Incorrigible, she smirked. "We do our best Marc."

Locally, it was a famous wedding, and a grand reception that Camille had organized. Towards the end of the reception Xavier introduced me to an older, well-dressed gentleman.

Xavier hesitated, like he was introducing a visiting dignitary. "Marc, this is Monsieur Olivier Lecuyer."

I got it—*Prieuré de Sion*

Xavier excused himself and scurried off to dance with Camille. Monsieur Lecuyer took me aside. He was casual, elegant, friendly and sophisticated. He was a man who was comfortable being in a command position. We chatted for awhile, and he asked me a few questions, which I answered, but I asked him none. I knew better. He wanted to know about my mother and my father. When I spoke I had his full attention. He listened with a kind of focus that was remarkable. I learned something important from observing the gentleman during that exchange. I realized that self-oriented individuals are the worst listeners. They will inevitably bring any topic back to themselves, and tend to misinterpret what others are trying to relate. Key words will set them off on all-too familiar tangents. This man was the opposite of a selfish person. Olivier Lecuyer was a service-to-others individual.

Presently, he looked over at Céline. "She is a remarkable woman. I apologize, I am taking up too much of your time. You probably want to dance with her."

"Yes," I said. "But I hope we can talk another time."

"I would enjoy that as well." He meant it. "One more thing—you will protect her—no?" He was dead serious, and conveying a message. Something for me to think about.

I looked into his eyes. They bore a resemblance to Céline's. "Yes sir, I certainly will."

Later, when we opened our wedding gifts, the gentleman had given us a full set of expensive Sabatier kitchen cutting knives, and six steak knives. Camille told me that the steak knives were reproductions of pocket knives that Napoleon gave to his top officers. Each knife featured a unique handle material: ebony, rosewood, ivory, olive, green and blue wood. Cast into the metal parts of each handle was the image of a golden honey bee, which she claimed was an important symbol of the Merovingian kings.

Also in the package was a nice, leather bound copy of an English translation of The Epic of Gilgamesh. It was an odd gift, and was obviously meant for me. A teacher had given me an assignment.

12

The Idyllic Life

Personally, I rather liked Father Bouchet. He was thoughtful, sensitive, and projected a kind of undeniable goodness that probably elicited love from some; while others may have perceived as a sign of weakness that could be taken advantage of. That quality made him very attractive to the young Mademoiselles. Several of them had obvious crushes for him, which he appeared to be oblivious to, or unaware of. He seemed to have boundless energy, bordering on hyperactivity.

Father Bouchet had arrived shortly before I had, earlier in the summer, having received the assignment to take over the diocese from the aging Father Durant; an icon who served for over fifty years. Due to some grumbling and disapproval from townsfolk, the young Father had been working hard to prove himself—too hard I thought.

One morning in late September Xavier announced that we would begin to harvest the grapes in the ripest of the vineyard blocks. That casual statement set the entire town into motion. Since I was a new arrival there, I observed it all with curiosity. It was a dedicated machine that had been performing the same task for so long it warranted minimal direction—like the mild tempered, slow moving draft horse they used to plow between the rows of vines.

The next morning, before sunrise, dressed in work cloths and a hat I knocked on Father Bouchet's door. It was crisp, cold, with the dew heavy on the cobblestones. He appeared in similar attire looking like he had just woke up, or not slept well.

"Good morning Robert." I purposefully used his given name. It was a risk, and a breach of formality, but he accepted it without chagrin. I was both taking him under my wing and offering him my friendship.

He glanced up at the sky with baggy eyes. *It's too early for a civilized man to get up.* "Good morning Marc."

The afternoon before, he had approached as Xavier and I were assessing the condition of the grapes.

He had addressed Xavier. "Monsieur Favreau. I would like to help with the grape harvest."

He was intimidated by Xavier.

Xavier was the most economically powerful man in the area and also the most blatantly pagan.

Xavier was gracious as always. "Of course, we need all the help we can get."

It was too easy. I could tell that Father Bouchet was out of his element and did not know how to proceed. I stepped up to the plate. "I will stop by and get you if you like—before sunrise."

"So early?"

Xavier added, "We need to bring the grapes in before they get too warm, or the wine will loose it's freshness..

We begin picking as early as we can see the clusters."

The next morning, Robert and I got into the car and drove to where a group of old men were preparing the equipment and the wine press. By the time we arrived we were both chilled, but the sun was just beginning to peek over the hills to the east. In the dry, rarefied early morning air my nose picked up the floral sugary fragrance of ripe fruit. I grabbed a sharpening stone and a couple of sharp sécateurs. The day before, several older men had gathered in the square to smoke, talk, and sharpen the curved knives.

We headed down to where Xavier and a middle aged matriarch were having a lively discussion—disagreeing about what order to pick the grapes in. They were not arguing—in fact they were both smirking. I had the distinct impression that this same exchange occurred every year. The ritual was obviously of greater importance than the arrival of Marc and Father Bouchet, because we were ignored for a time, until they paused so Xavier could assign us each a row. I spent the time stroking "Dauphin", the draft horse, who was hitched up to a large wagon.

"Good morning," Xavier said. "You two can start on the top of these two rows here."

We headed up there with our baskets, each walking in our own row next to the chest-high vines.

I queried, "Have you picked grapes before?"

"No, this will be my first time."

"Me too. There are no vineyards where I grew up."

"And where was that?"

"Near Seattle."

He questioned me about my background. He was genuinely interested, so I responded by telling him all about the Puget Sound, the fish, and the beauty of Mt. Rainier National Park. Eventually as we picked, the conversation reversed directions and I queried about his childhood.

Father Bouchet was from Calais, a port town in the far north of France that had been pummeled during the war. He was from a pious family, but his father had sent him off to seminary to get him out of harms way, and because he was the third of three sons. In parts of France, inheritance laws were English style, since the British had controlled those regions at one time. The first born son would legally inherit the lands and the titles, which left the younger sons to fend for themselves. It was not unusual for the second and third sons to become priests or soldiers.

He was more than willing to talk. I realized that as "Father Bouchet", he had plenty of duties and people to take care of, but "Robert" spent his evenings alone. Working next to someone of the same mind all day can cause an entire gamut of topics to be entertained. I picked a bit faster than he did, so had to pause or slow down to stay next to him. After awhile Xavier came down to check on us. We were probably not picking as fast as the others, but he said nothing. I think he was pleased that Father Bouchet and I were getting along well.

At lunch time we all assembled in the town square. Tables had been set up in the shade, and food had been prepared by the women who were too old to be picking in the hot sun. The simple fare was laid out on the tables: leek soup, loaves of fresh bread, big chunks of hard cheese, and the vin de presse wine from the previous year. The men spoke in their rough dialect; children ran around playing, the mothers scolding them for this or that. It was the first time I had eaten with the local townsfolk. Robert and I were quiet—observing it all.

Céline showed up and sat down with us. She had been picking grapes for Xavier's personal cuvée in the ripest part of the vineyard. She had been working hard, and was unusually lively and animated. Robert was pleased, but visibly stiffened and became more formal. Robert was attracted to her, but Father Bouchet was intimidated by her. If Xavier was the most blatant pagan, then Céline was the epitome of it.

It wasn't really a truth picture—I just figured it out. He was reasonably comfortable in the presence of women, unless she was a woman he happened to be attracted to. It was a little like the enigma of the duplicity of the Catholic dogma itself: Women are viewed as sinners and lesser than men, while in a kind of vague contrast there is the persistent veneration of the Virgin Mary, the Magdalene, and the Black Madonna—which are obviously carry-overs from the goddess worship era.

Céline fit squarely in the goddess camp, but here she was eating, joking with us and chiding him by reaching over and pushing on his arm. He drank it up like he hadn't had water for a week. He also drank a bit more wine than he intended, and was a little tipsy when we headed back towards our picking baskets. Afterwards he became thoughtful, and we worked in silence for awhile. Eventually I brought up the subject of improving the town. It was more businesslike; and I was addressing him as Father Bouchet. He had been thinking along the same lines, but did not know how to get the money to do so. I offered to provide the funding for a few projects.

The first project we discussed was obvious:

Probably the oldest lady in town, Madame Dupuis, lived off of a tiny pension. When she was younger, she had lived and worked in Paris during the "gay 90's", and had rubbed shoulders with some of the famous impressionist painters. Now, her front door was literally falling off of its hinges, but she was probably too proud to accept help from the likes of me. I didn't know how to approach her. Father Bouchet claimed he could manage it. Between the two of us, we formed a village improvement alliance.

I also began working on the house project. There was a large limestone quarry below the town, so I found a couple of out-of-work quarrymen to help me before the winter snows set in. We drilled holes and blasted away at the bottom of the cliff, and I hired some local teenagers to help clear away the debris. I worked right along with everyone. I enjoyed it, but it also served to give me some respect from the locals.

In the spring the house project resumed, and I was ready with some materials. Due to the war, building materials in France were still in short supply. While working at the Boeing company, I had encountered two new building materials: plywood and insulation. Neither were yet available in France, so I ordered a shipping container full from New York, and had it shipped to Marseilles. The insulation was made of spun gypsum, and I was pleasantly surprised when I found that the plywood bore a stamp from Rosedale, Oregon.

The only problem was that both the plywood and the insulation were designed to work around the English measuring system. The French workmen almost revolted. They were only familiar with the metric system, and to a lesser extent, the old Royal French Foot, which was different than the English Foot.

I resorted to hiring an American carpenter I had met in a café in Avignon on my return from the docks in Marseilles. He was a decent enough guy, but a bit of a wild card.

The carpenter's name was Brian O'Reilly, and was from California, where his father worked as a home builder. Like myself, Brian had served as a soldier in France, but he was one of those guys that had some rough experiences here during the war. In a nutshell, he had left part of his childhood in France, and was now back here trying to recover it. He was prone to violent mood swings and binge drinking.

In spite of that, I liked him. He had a funny, sarcastic sense of humor, and when he was on the job he was skilled and worked efficiently. Unfortunately, he often-times didn't get along with others well; especially the other workman, who had an agenda to shun him.

Therefore, I worked along with Brian as well as a local seventeen year-old laborer by the name of Pierre. Brian was almost hostile towards the others, but some-how he liked Pierre, probably because the boy didn't seem to have a mean bone in his body. When Brian got upset, Pierre simply wouldn't react, so the boy served as a stabilizing factor for the temperamental Irish-American carpenter. Brian responded by being patient and kind to Pierre, and spent time teaching him techniques.

One way or another, since we built the walls "California" style, it all happened very quickly. We would frame a wall on the floor, nail the plywood on, and then stand it up in place. The French carpenters did good work, but their method was much slower. They protested, claiming that the building would not hold up over time.

Brian did not even attempt to defend his choice of techniques. He responded by simply telling them to "fuck off!" He was in the habit of using swear words proudly, loudly, and often. He even went out of his way to learn their French equivalents.

In spite of all of that I still liked him, perhaps because he was so raw that it was refreshing. Unlike the rest of us, he didn't seem to care what anyone thought about him.

One day, while we were having lunch together on the job site, I felt compelled to probe. In good humor, I inquired. "So Brian, why are you so intense all of the time? I've never known anyone so volatile."

He chewed on his sandwich and surveyed me for a moment. I was pushing it, but he knew I liked him. "You know I am a triple Aries," he proclaimed calmly.

"I don't know anything about astrology," I said.

"What day were you born on?"

" January twenty first," I answered.

"Okay, that makes you an Aquarian, at least by your sun sign. There's also your rising sign and your moon sign. You may be something like Sagittarius rising with a Leo Moon." He waved his hands around, still holding the sandwich. "It all has to do with mathematics and trigonometry. Not many people have all three aspects in one sign. I have all three in Aries."

I wasn't sure whether I believed in astrology or not. Later that evening at dinner with the family, I brought it up. Neither of the women had met Brian. With all of those four-letter words, he was not the kind of guy you invited to a dinner party, but they had certainly heard about him in the evenings after I got home. Brian was like the antagonist in a Shakespeare comedy. When they learned that he was a triple Aries they were surprised. The Favreaus were well versed in astrology.

The next day Céline showed up to see the new chateau—at least that's what she claimed. I think she really wanted to meet the triple Aries—like visiting a rare animal in a zoo. She hadn't been there since we started. The framing was almost completed, and Brian, Pierre, and I were laying the plywood on the roof. A job site is usually an all-male environment. When a woman enters the area the energy automatically changes. All of the men instinctively become acutely aware of her. It clearly illustrates how men need to be near, and gravitate towards female energy.

When she arrived, Brian flipped into a completely different mode and became surprisingly civil, to the point of being charming. Céline joked with him, thanked him for helping, and complemented him on his work. She climbed a ladder up to the second floor to survey the master bedroom suite. I had incorporated a half-tower into the house design. On the main floor, the dining room was in the lower part of the tower, with windows circling almost 180 degrees. It featured a superb territorial view. Directly above the dining room was the master bedroom, where the upper part of the tower served as a place we could relax in the evenings and watch the sunset. Céline was pleased.

Two days later the framing was completed, so I drove Brian O'Reilly to the train station, gave him a bonus, and bid him farewell. I have no doubt that the French craftsmen gossiped about him for years afterwards—less than admirably. At least he was not forgotten.

By September we had completed the house. It featured

maple flooring throughout, and matching maple cabinets. There had been extra room in the shipping container from New York, so I had the company add easily enough maple flooring and hardwood boards for the house along with the plywood. With the off-white walls, and the elaborate white molding the effect was one of lightness and warmth.

Shortly after we moved in we invited Camille and Xavier up for a celebratory dinner. The finish carpenters had built in a lighted China cabinet in the hallway between the kitchen and the dining room. I asked Camille if she would mind getting some wine glasses out of it.

"Marc, is this your mother's tea set?" Camille and Céline were examining it. Camille knew all about fine China.

"Yes, I've had it stored in the cellar," I answered.

"It's eighteenth century Austrian," she said. "Quite valuable. Museum pieces really. They were made by the same artisan who Marie Antoinette favored. I can understand why your mother refused to let you touch them!"

Céline stared at me with an implacable look.

Who was your mother anyway?

That evening Camille had brought another bottle of her favorite Burgundy from Musigny. They were running low on it, and our cellar needed to be stocked as well. It gave me an idea.

"Xavier, why don't we make some red wine that the ladies would like?" I said. "Is it hard to make?"

He shrugged his shoulders. "Not hard, no. We would need a barrel."

"Do you know anywhere we can get some good Pinot Noir grapes?"

He thought about it. "I do have an old friend. Martin Bruyères, a vigneron in Mercurey. I haven't spoken with him since...well since before the war."

I could almost hear the wheels begin to turn inside of his head. Eventually Xavier became excited about the idea of both making some red wine and seeing his old friend again.

Two weeks later, immediately after we got the white grapes in, pressed and the juice into tanks, Xavier and I climbed into the Mercedes and headed northwest towards Mercurey.

It was a full afternoon of driving, but one that resides in my memory with fondness. We were blessed with a clear warm day with which to cruise through the countryside.

Xavier didn't get out much. If he ventured out too far in his old car he tended to get lost, and some of the roads and bridges were still being repaired from the war. I don't think he'd been on a road trip in years. He made the most of it—excitable, almost like a child. When we would pass workers in the fields picking fruit or grapes he would hang out of the car and proclaim, "I love France. I love my country. You're beautiful!" He blew kisses to the pickers, who would shake their heads or smile. One gentleman gave us a renaissance bow. The car's convertible top had disintegrated long ago. I had fastened little French flags on the front fenders, which fluttered in the wind and made us look like visiting dignitaries—a rolling comedy team—the ambassadors of wine. We drank a bottle of his Altesse right out of the bottle on the way. The ambassadors don't need cups—we're men!

By the time we pulled in to Mercurey we were in pure form. We were greeted by Madame Bruyères, who was wearing an apron.

"Xavier!" She spread her arms up and out, and turned her cheek for him to kiss. She reached up and tousled his hair.

"What happened to your hair?"

"It's all gray now," he said. "What can I say? You haven't aged a bit Giselle. Still a vision of loveliness."

"Oh stop it Xavier." She soaked it up.

"This is Marc Rémillard, Céline's husband."

" Little Céline. She was always so shy."

"Well, she's quite tall now Madame," I said.

"Yes, I suppose so." She looked over her shoulder. "I must get back into the kitchen. I'm preparing a wonderful meal for us. It will be ready in a half an hour. I think Martin is working on the equipment. Don't let him take you into the vineyard. Do you promise?"

"I promise," replied Xavier, holding a finger up.

Martin took us into the vineyard. They couldn't help themselves. It was what these men truly loved. The plan was for us to pick our grapes the following morning, haul them home, and get them crushed and into a fermenter by the evening.

We walked through the vineyard block Martin claimed was ready to pick, tasting and assessing the ripeness of the grapes as we went. They were old, short, gnarled vines with trunks the size of my forearm. The sweet grapes began to go to my head.

Forty minutes later I was hungry and tapped on my Patek Phillipe. "Gentlemen, we promised Madame Bruyères we would be in for dinner ten minutes ago."

"Oh yes, she has been working hard on this meal," Martin said, with a little trepidation.

Luckily, out timing was perfect. When we arrived, she had just set out a cheese plate and a cool bottle of their Pinot Gris. It was a positively gourmet meal: with linen, fine China, and silverware. The lady could really cook, and she had gone all out for the rare visit from Xavier.

The three of them had much to catch up on, so I was quiet, enjoying the superb meal and Martin's excellent red wine. It was not quite as structural and full bodied as Camille and Céline's favorites from Musigny and Gevrey-Chambertin, but was very enjoyable nonetheless. The good news was that our timing was auspicious: Martin claimed that it could be the best year for his grapes in a decade.

Partway through the meal he unexpectedly put his hands on the table and said, "You know, I really think we should wait one more day to begin picking the old vines. I sense no rain on the horizon, and one more warm day should help the flavors pull together, with more complexity!" He paused and continued, "The fruit from the young vines in the lower block is ready to pick though. We can do that tomorrow and get it into a fermenter." He looked at Xavier. "What do you say Xavier? Can you and Marc stay with us for one more day?"

It was a master stroke. Yes, he was a good vigneron, and wanted to make the best wine he could; but he was also maneuvering so that the old friends could spend just a little more time together. I added that bit of wisdom to my mental diary. Friendship is rare; savor it when you can.

Li Bai, the famous Chinese poet had expressed a similar idea twelve-hundred years before:

If life smiles at you,
Enjoy it completely.
Never let the golden cup
Wait in the moonlight

The next day I experienced first-hand the process of getting red grapes into a fermenter. I offered to be Martin's personal assistant for the day so I could learn as much as I could. We picked, sorted, crushed, and secured the precious grapes into one large vat. We got done early, so by the time Madame Bruyères came home we were already sitting in the shade enjoying some Pinot Gris.

She had been out doing charity work, and was perplexed at having to cook for the four of us.

I gathered she was the kind of person that could only do things one way—full on. In the middle of the day, when Martin was dealing with the pickers, I had driven into town and bought the last of the day's fresh bread, some cheese, sausage, and a kilo of green olives. There was also quite a bit of food in the refrigerator from the last night's meal. Still she flustered. Serving guests leftovers? It just wasn't proper! We didn't care. The ambassadors of wine seized the moment. Xavier and I got down on our knees and *begged* for the leftovers. Both speaking at once, we pleaded, "Please Madame Bruyères, I have been craving another taste of the boeuf Bourguignon all day!"—"Giselle, I know there is more vichysousse in the refrigerator. You are cruel not to offer us some!" We went on until we were all laughing, especially old Martin. He laughed until tears were pouring down his cheeks. He couldn't get over it either; how his old friend Xavier and the young Rémillard had got down on their knees and shamelessly begged for leftovers.

When I went in to clean up for dinner, scrub as I might, I couldn't get the stain from the red grapes off of my hands, and complained about it when I got to the table. Martin solemnly stood up and raised his glass to me.

With gravity, he addressed me. "Marc Rémillard,

I would like to initiate you into a holy order!"

The Prieuré de Sion?

He paused dramatically. "You are now of the Order of the Purple Hand!" They guffawed. It was an old joke. Okay, tease me if you will. Have your fun. I begrudgingly accepted being the butt of their joke.

That excursion with Xavier secured another special place in my memory. Now I hold it close, another of those gilded moments in time that I remember and refer to. What is really sacred? Some holy artifact or special place? Gauging by my own personal response, I would put the adventure to Mercurey with Xavier up against any pilgrimage or visit to a holy site. Is our divinity defined by what we aspire to be, or rather by what we actually do?

The next morning we picked our grapes, bade farewell to our gracious hosts and headed out. The poor Mercedes was overloaded, scraping on the pavement in places. I had removed the back seat long ago, and now we had wooden boxes of grapes stacked high up behind us, and stuffed into the trunk.

We drove mostly in silence. Xavier's mood had changed. He was still taking everything in; savoring the sights and the fragrances of the harvest and forests, but his vivacity was gone. It was all tinged with a kind of thoughtful, noble sadness. Since I had met him his mental health had not improved. He was gradually becoming more forgetful, but he was wise. He didn't say it, but I think he suspected that was probably the last time he would see Martin and Giselle.

When we pulled into town the sun was just setting, displaying a marvelous autumn red that illuminated the canopy of leaves on the tops of the vines in Xavier's vineyards.

"Your vines are the most beautiful of all Xavier!"

"Yes, all of my children are happy...except one." He had his head turned away, looking out towards his vineyards. I didn't press it, but I felt that I understood. I had been there over a year, and Jacques had not made an appearance.

We didn't have a crushing machine for red grapes, so we did it the old-fashioned way—with our feet. The ladies did most of the stomping, while we removed some of the stems from the clusters. The rest we just threw in whole. Father Bouchet helped, and it became kind of a party. Céline pulled Yvette up into the vat, so she could feel the squishy grapes between her toes. By the time it was over I was exhausted.

The next morning I was compelled to check on the wine early. I had bought a new, small oak fermenter just large enough to make wine to fill one barrel, and a new barrel to transfer the fermented wine into. I began to understand the lure of the winemaker. I fussed over that fermenter like it was a child, visiting it several times per day to submerge the grapes into the liquid and keep the fruit flies at bay. That batch of wine became my baby. When it began to ferment two days later it was exciting—frothing, foaming and giving off an array of strange smells. Xavier was glad to have me take charge of the project, and said that the fermentation was proceeding well. Three weeks later we transferred the wine into the 225 liter barrel. I was pleased. Twenty-five cases of good Mercurey Pinot Noir should keep the ladies happy!

That winter we received an unusually large snow fall, but spent the cold season comfortable in our new home.

By April the snow gradually turned to rain in the mountains, and twisting ropes of solid ice and deep snow melted into eager streams of bone-chilling water that hurried down through the mountain meadows towards their big sister, the Rhône river, which rose to its banks before pouring into the Mediterranean sea. The water of the sacred spring was joined by the snow melt, which ignored the delicate whirlpool behind the l'ermitage ancienne, flowing over it before gushing over the cliff to form a proud waterfall behind the tiny cottage.

By the time the last of the snow melted I was more than ready for the warmth and luxurious greenery of spring. In late May the newspaper reported that there was to be a week of unusually warm weather on the Mediterranean coast, so I decided it would be a good time to take Monique to the beach. Amongst the society of children, the love of warm, sunny, sandy beaches is unanimous; and Monique was yet to experience it. I grew up with the rocky Puget Sound beaches and had visited the expansive Pacific beaches many times. Since I was honor bound to perform my parental duty, from an advertisement in the newspaper I booked a hotel for three days at the French Riviera.

Céline had always refused to ride in the German car. My investments were doing well, so I decided to trade it in for a new French one. I could afford a nice car, and American cars were available, but when I visited the dealerships I was amazed at the sheer size of the 1949's. The Buicks, Packards, Hudsons, Lincolns and Cadillacs were enormous. I wasn't sure how they would squeeze onto some of the narrow French roads. They were like huge, stylish, bulbous loaves of bread going down the road. It seemed the idea was that one could be enjoying the comfort of relaxing on one's sofa while barrelling down the highway at the same time. I had become weary of the spectacle that my German car presented, so I chose a smaller French model.

The day after I brought the new car home we loaded it up and headed out, following the Rhône river as it flowed south towards the Mediterranean sea. Eventually we left the river and headed east towards Provence. Monique was at an age where she was really beginning to observe and process new environments.

It was an enjoyable vacation. The four star hotel in the Riviera was more expensive and luxurious than I had realized, and featured a casino, which neither Céline or I were interested in, but we relaxed into it. It was a good time to be vacationing because the bulk of the summer tourists had not arrived yet. Most importantly—as predicted, Monique was in heaven on the beach.

On the return trip home we had a fun assignment from Camille. She wanted two cases of wine from Domaine Tempier, which was near the Riviera. We drove uphill through the dry, rocky countryside near Bandol. It was a Mediterranean climate, with pines, old olive trees and the last of the drying, colorful spring wildflowers. We were greeted by a lady by the name of Lulu, who remembered Camille. She was very engaging, fussed over Monique and let us taste the wine. It was so good that I decided we could squeeze two more cases into the car for our cellar.

The side excursion was rewarding, but since it took up part of the day, we drove until we decided to stay in a small town near Lyon for the night. I was almost out of cash, not realizing how much a vacation like that could cost, so I decided we would go into Geneva the next day before returning home.

13

Premonition

The next day when we arrived in Geneva, Raoul was not in the bank. I knew better than to inquire about his whereabouts in the bank, so I knocked on Davide's door. When he saw me his eyes went wide. He shut the door and stepped outside with me.

"Marc, what are you doing here?"

"What do you mean?" I said. "I was just in the bank, and Raoul wasn't there."

"He's in the hospital." Davide stared at me. "He was tortured...They were looking for you!"

"What? Tortured...by whom?"

"I don't know, but they were asking questions about you. Two men. He thinks they might have killed him if his neighbor hadn't come to the door with her dog."

"That doesn't make any sense!" I said.

"They have him under guard now, but I got to talk to him before the guard arrived. The police probably want to question you."

I wasn't in the mood, so I took my family through the small border crossing I frequented, where the guards recognized me, and let us through without question. Before leaving Geneva, I had put Monique in the car and quietly told Céline what had transpired concerning Raoul outside of the car.

We were almost home, and had just passed the l'ermitage ancienne when Monique began to cry. Céline turned around. "What's wrong honey?" She took one look at Monique. "Marc, stop the car."

We both looked back at her. She was panting and crying. "There are bad men at the chateau!" She said between sobs. "Find uncle Xavier!"

"Back up!" Céline commanded. I backed up and turned into the l'ermitage ancienne. When I parked, the car was not visible from the road. I fished my pistol out from underneath the seat. Céline got Monique out and coaxed us into the back where the whirlpool was. We were thirsty after the long drive, and the water helped us think and reconnoiter. It was odd. Céline took charge of the situation. I had never seen her in that mode before.

"You need to go check on Xavier," she told me.

"I don't want to leave you and Monique here alone."

"I know where to hide if we need to...Hurry!"

Somehow, I felt she was right, and ran down the trail, past the sacred spring, the pool, and into the open back door of the house.

Xavier was laying on his back in the dining room with his eyes open. There was a small pool of blood behind his head.

"Xavier!" I knelt down next to him. Xavier was gone. I put my hand on his chest. His body was still warm. I closed my eyes, as if it was just a bad dream I could wake up from. Immediately, I saw a brief picture in my mind of two men, one with red hair. "No, not Xavier!" I started to feel emotional but realized it was a luxury that I simply couldn't allow myself to indulge in yet. I forced myself to squelch it. Instead I got up, checked through the window to see if there was a car outside, and searched the house. It was empty, but there was a note in Camille's stationary on the table.

Xavier

Remember I am taking the train to Paris today as I told you this morning. My sister is ill. I will be back in about a week. There is food in the refrigerator you can heat up, and Céline can cook for you too. They should be back from their vacation soon.

Love,

Camille

That made me think of my two gentle, defenseless ladies waiting at the l'ermitage ancienne. They were in danger. It frightened me. I panicked and ran out the back door and up the trail. Going up was not nearly as easy as coming down. I had to stop at the spring to catch my breath. I was not in very good physical condition after a winter of being snowed in. When I reached the top I was relieved to find Céline waiting on the bench and Monique playing in the whirlpool with bits of sticks and floating flowers. Céline followed as I moved through the cottage and out into the front where the car was. Panting, I didn't know what to say. I didn't know how to tell her.

Suddenly, she looked like the woman I had found huddling in the corner of a cold stone cellar.

"They murdered him didn't they?"

I couldn't speak, I just nodded. She turned her head to the side. Her lower lip began to quiver and her eyes fluttered; and then she steeled up, just as I had.

Almost too calmly, she quietly said, "We must leave here. We will go to Lyon and find Jacques."

"Jacques?"

"He will know what to do."

"What about the police?"

"They are of no help. Informants. We would then be stationary and vulnerable."

"Informants? What are you talking about?" I was baffled. She moved closer and took my hands in hers, much like when I did the same with her hands that first time at the sacred spring.

"Do you trust me?" She asked.

I nodded quickly.

"Please take us to Lyon."

"Okay."

She softened and replied, "Okay." It had become a private joke between us. She hugged me. The woman never fully relaxed, but here she was wound up like a coil spring.

Before leaving, we filled our water jug. I walked out to the road to make sure there was not a car coming. It felt like the first time I had been there, hiding behind a tree from the Germans. I listened—there was only birdsong, high in the trees.

It was a two-hour drive back to Lyon. We had been driving all day. When Monique finally fell asleep in the back seat I turned to Céline.

"Perhaps there are a few things you should tell me."

She was leaning against her door, and looked out of

the passenger window. The woman held on to her secrets like a dragon guarding her horde of jewels.

"It was the ritual assassination," she said flatly.

"What? What the hell are you talking about?"

"Don't swear with me!" She was prickly. The dragon instinctively resented divulging even a tiny bit of her horde. I said nothing, and waited. It had to come out—like a tide.

Eventually, in a different voice she admitted, "They killed my parents, and my first husband Jean."

I sensed two different emotional issues: sorrow and loss for the death of her parents; and resentment, pain and loss with Jean. Except for Camille and Xavier mentioning him, I knew very little about her first husband. As a guy, I hadn't really wanted to know, so I had never pressed it, but Céline was like a closed book on the issue. Since it was a very delicate situation, I decided to steer it away from the emotional and towards the historical.

"So who are we talking about? Who killed your parents?" I didn't mention Jean.

The dragon huffed, looked out the window again and paused. "Religious fanatics. They have been after us for over a thousand years."

I put two and two together. "You mean the Roman Catholic Church hunts members of the Prieuré de Sion?"

"Yes and no. In the olden days, there was no question that the directive came from the hierarchy of the church. Look at the Inquisition, and the Albigensian crusade. But now they probably have nothing to do with it. They can however, conveniently choose to turn a blind eye when a fanatical rogue order that associates themselves with the church commits murder."

She paused and added, "There have been other groups after us as well."

"A *ritual* murder?"

"They used to mark the victim with one of their signs for the devil. They stopped that long ago to keep themselves off of the radar of the police," she said. "Now they are more discreet."

She started to cry, so I questioned her no further.

We soon began to enter the outskirts of the city. "Where shall we go in Lyon?" I asked.

"Jacques is an urbanite. We will find him in the heart of the city—where most of both the wealth and the corruption is."

It was an odd thing for her to say, but once I met Jacques it made more sense. Céline and I are alike in one important way: even though some of the finest facets of life (art and music for example) can be experienced in cities, we both feel more comfortable when surrounded by nature. When we have entertained visitors from the city, I've noticed how uncomfortable they can become when they are out of town, and particularly fearful of what they perceive to be the wild forest. In contrast, I feel the safest when I am in the forest.

We stopped and consulted a map. I could tell where the oldest part of the city was because the streets were close together. We drove there and rented a hotel room. Monique was still asleep, so I carried her up and put her on one of the beds, sat down in a chair at the little hotel table next to the window. Out of her purse, Céline produced a small telephone book that I had never seen before and dialed a number on the smudged black telephone that sat in front of me. Since she was standing

116

next to me, I could hear Jacques voice on the other end of the line.

"Jacques, it's Céline."

"What's wrong?" *She wouldn't call him unless there was a problem.*

She paused. "They took Xavier. They took your father."

She waited. "The ritual?" Jacques finally asked.

"I believe so. Marc found him in the house."

"Where is my mother?"

"Very fortunate. She's on her way to Paris on the train to visit Véronique. She may be there by now."

"Where are you?" He asked.

"We are in Lyon."

"We?"

"Marc, our daughter Monique and I. We had to flee."

"Where in Lyon?" I pushed the worn hotel literature towards her.

"Uh...At the Hotel Tolbert on Rue Chalopin, near Rue Saint-Michel," she replied.

"You are not safe there. I will come get you," He hung up.

Céline replaced the receiver, lifted her eyebrows and said under her breath, "Jacques! I love him but he can be so rude." She plopped down on the bed.

Olivier Lecuyer stepped into his study carrying a large manila envelope in his left hand. Standing behind his desk, he opened the top drawer and pulled out a wide sable artists brush and a rosewood handled violin-makers knife. After cutting the top of the envelope with the knife, he drew out the contents and placed it squarely on the polished desk. It was a piece of cardboard with a sheet of waxed paper taped to it. He carefully sliced through the waxed paper and peeled it back. Beneath was what appeared to be an ordinary letter except that it was written on handmade paper, with bits of fiber still showing. The text was brief, composed with a fountain pen and covering the top half of the page:

Dear Olivier

We have finally completed the translation of *The Red Lion* from Hungarian. It is an absolutely superb story. I had to force myself to put it down at night just so I would get some sleep. It is difficult to describe the profound effect it has had on me.

Blanche and I will be coming through Lyon next month, and will bring you a copy. We are looking forward to seeing you again.

Your devoted friend,

Serge

Olivier smiled, reached for a bottle of cognac and proceeded to pour a little into a brandy balloon next to it. He dipped the artists brush into the glass, applied some cognac to the lower half of the letter then set the brush on the rim of the glass to dry.

The telephone rang. He ignored it, staring down at the letter. Slowly, gray letters began to appear, written in the same hand as the letter above. He sat down and read the message under the desk lamp. The telephone rang again. This time, he turned and stared at it. *Jacques.* Even though he already had a knack for it, he had been perfecting the art of knowing who was calling prior to picking up the receiver.

"Jacques?" He listened, consternation coming to his face, "Yes, of course." He set the receiver down, closed his eyes for a moment before looking towards the window on the other side of the room. He looked down at the letter. The message on the bottom half had completely disappeared. He dropped it into the trash bin. Finally he got up, poured a glass of wine, lit a candle and placed it on his desk. He sat down in the office chair and solemnly raised the glass to the candle.

Thirty minutes after Céline phoned Jacques there was a knock on the hotel door.

Céline stood up. I moved to the side of the door, pointed my pistol head high, and quickly opened the door. It was Jacques, but not the same dashing, vibrant young man whose photo graced his mother's bureau. This Jacques was in his thirties, but looked like he was twenty years older than that. His face was sallow, lined, with dark bags under his eyes, and a knife scar on one side of his forehead. Seeing Céline, he ignored the pistol, and pushed past me towards her. A cloud of stale cigarette smoke and body odor followed him into the room.

They hugged. Céline, with her hands on his shoulders reached up and moved some hair with her thumb from his forehead in an affectionate, preening gesture, stood up on her toes and kissed him next to her thumb. I couldn't see his face.

"I am so sorry Jacques," she said.

"It's not your fault."

Lets put all social graces aside, shall we?

Jacques is Céline's cousin. His father just died. He is trying to help us! It was a mantra I found myself using

119

many times afterwards to keep myself from punching him.

"Let's go. I will take you somewhere safer," he said.

"Where?" Céline asked.

"You'll see."

I picked up our sleeping, warm rubber child and followed them down the stairs and into the street.

"I'll drive," he said. "I know the way."

I handed him the keys as Céline got into the back seat. I held Monique in the passenger seat. Jacques drove my new car through the narrow streets like a maniac, missing other cars by what seemed like millimeters. He would brake suddenly, forcing me to hold Yvette's head to keep it from bouncing around violently.

I repeated the mantra. Fortunately we did not have far to go. In a mixed residential neighborhood he pulled up to an industrial metal garage door, got out, and looked around before inserting a key into a keyhole next to the door. It began to roll up automatically. I was impressed. Twenty years later electric garage door openers became more common, but in 1949 they were rare. When we pulled in, the door slowly closed automatically. There was already a car in the building, with room for perhaps two more.

We got out and climbed an industrial concrete stairway that was clean and painted, and came to a metal door. Jacques pushed the doorbell, which looked like an elevator control button. The door was opened by Monsieur Olivier Lecuyer, the gentleman I had been introduced to at our wedding.

Monsieur Lecuyer was very gracious. "Marc, Céline, please come in. Oh—a sleeping princess!" He whispered,

"Let's bring Monique in here." *He remembered her name.*

We followed him down a hallway on a thick Persian-style runner, and into an ornate room with elaborate molding painted in cream and gold.

"I hope you don't mind Rococo. My dear wife wanted one room done in the style, since we had the furniture to match. It's the only room I have with two beds."

Are you kidding. It looked like we had just walked into a bedroom in Louis the sixteenth's summer palace. The furnishings were real. We put Monique into one of the beds, turned the light off, but left the door open. He led us into his study. The decor of the house was luxurious, but it was not designed for entertaining. It felt like an ultra-comfortable, deluxe refuge. Jacques was already there, in a chair next to an open window on the far side of the room. I gathered it was a habitual posture for him; smoking and watching the street below like a hawk.

"Please, sit down, you must be tired." The gentleman gestured towards a mohair sofa while he poured three glasses of port. He handed one to Céline, one to me, and set the other on a marble table next to a leather chair. He did not offer port to Jacques.

"I am sorry to hear about Xavier," he said as he settled into his chair. "Unfortunately, we must deal with the unpleasant business first." He continued, "Marc, how did you find Xavier?"

I had been trying to ignore that image in my mind.
"I went in through the back door of the house, and Xavier was right there on the dining room floor on his back. He had been shot through the head with a small caliber bullet."

"Yes, their most current method," Monsieur Lecuyer said, with resignation.

Jacques, still looking out the window asked, "Did anyone see you enter the house?"

I thought about it. "No, I don't think so."

"Where was your car?"

"Up at the l'ermitage ancienne, where I left Céline and Yvette."

"You went down the trail?" Jacques asked.

"Yes." I tried to imagine Jacques, a heavy smoker, going up that steep trail.

Monsieur LeCuyer held up a hand to Jacques. "Why did you go to the l'ermitage ancienne?" *He knew about the place.*

I looked over at Céline, who said, "We were almost home, when Monique began to cry. She claimed there were 'bad men at the chateau'."

"So we went to the l'ermitage ancienne instead," I added.

The gentleman raised his eyebrows. "Talented child!" He took a sip of his port, "So...as far as the police are concerned, you are still on a holiday, and have not yet returned home."

I got it. "Yes...yes, no one saw us."

"Good, but Xavier is still probably laying there in the dark in his home," he said.

Jacques piped up again, "We don't know that for sure."

"True...so let's form a strategy." Monsieur Lecuyer thought about it. "First, Céline could call the house to check in on Xavier. If the police are there they will answer the telephone. If not, is there someone you could call to check in on Xavier?"

"But that is deceptive!" Céline said. She had an almost zealot-like honest streak.

No one replied. I think she realized how unpractical her attitude was even as she was expressing it.

"Father Bouchet," I said. "I hate to do that to him."

"Perhaps he's involved already!" Jacques blurted out.

"No...no," Céline and I both said at the same time.

"Sounds like a good job for a priest to me. Their religion is all about *death* anyway!"

"Jacques!" Monsieur Lecuyer held his hand up again. Jacques sulked and smoked nervously.

Céline made the calls. There was no answer at the house. She apologized for troubling Father Bouchet when she reached him, and was quite convincing. The priestess lied gracefully, but didn't like doing it.

Afterwards, we sipped our port in silence for awhile.

"I just don't understand why this has happened," I said. "Céline told me about what she called 'the ritual assassination' as we were driving here, but I can't grasp why anyone would want to kill Xavier."

"Revenge," Jacques stated flatly.

Monsieur Lecuyer didn't counter. "How much do you know about the Prieuré de Sion, Marc?"

"Not much really. Xavier told me that it is a secret society dedicated to the evolvement of mankind in general. And then my friend Raoul..."

"Raoul!" Céline said. "We forgot about Raoul!"

We told them what had occurred in Geneva earlier that day.

Monsieur Lecuyer still maintained control of the conversation. "So what did Raoul tell you about the Prieuré de Sion?"

"I don't know if I should tell you. It's not particularly flattering."

"Please...I am not easily insulted."

"How did he put it?... 'The Prieuré de Sion is one of the many secret societies in Europe with delusions of grandeur. It's kind of a wealthy gentleman's club that is obsessed with the notion of being old French royalty.' He also used the terms 'fanatical', and 'heretics' in his description."

The gentleman chuckled, "Your friend Raoul expresses himself well. How did he know of the Priory in the first place?"

"His brother is in the Swiss Guard." I felt Jacques eyes boring into me.

"So we can assume that if Raoul is free enough in his speech to relate to you what his brother said, then he in turn may also have told his brother that he knows someone involved in the Priory."

I could understand his reasoning. "But Raoul's brother wouldn't condone the torture of his own brother."

"Of course not, but he may have gathered information that was shared with others. Information is gathered and traded amongst intelligence agencies like a currency, oftentimes in blocks." Monsieur Lecuyer pointed out. "A list of names of members of the Prieuré de Sion would be valuable to groups intent on eliminating enemies of the church."

"Is the Prieuré de Sion an enemy of the church?"

"No, at least not from our perspective. Since the inception of the order we have maintained a policy of non-aggression." He glanced over at Jacques and made a little face—pursing his lips together. "At least for the exceptional rogue members." He took another sip of port and continued, "There are various chapters in the Priory with differing philosophies. The 'Roman' chapter is much more aligned with the Catholic church than the French chapter."

"But the church itself considers the Priory as an enemy?"

"Historically, yes."

"Why?"

The gentleman sat back in his chair, "The key question, the answers to which warrant lengthy discussions. Would you consider continuing this discussion tomorrow?"

"Yes sir, I think it is time I know what's going on."

14

The Shield Bearer

The next morning Monique woke up early. I could have used more sleep, but by habit I got up with her. Monsieur Lecuyer was an early riser as well, and appeared with the morning newspaper in hand shortly after we got up. When I introduced Monique to our host, she gave him just a hint of a little curtsy. I don't know where she had learned that but the gentleman beamed. "Enchanté Mademoiselle," he said with exaggerated formality.

"Papa, I'm hungry. Could we have hash browns and eggs?"

"We will have something." We'd missed dinner the night before.

"What are hash browns?" Our host inquired.

"Fried potatoes. I am in the habit of cooking big American-style breakfasts for Monique and myself. Sometimes I will fry them in olive oil and bits of bacon with cheese melted on top."

"Oh!" He exclaimed. "What can I do to be so fortunate as to be included in this ritual?"

I chuckled. "I'd be more than happy to cook for all of us sir. I enjoy cooking actually."

"That is a blessing. Since my wife passed away several years ago I have struggled with it. I do make a superb cup of coffee though. I buy only the best of beans, and grind them myself."

"Are we a team then?" I asked.

"Absolutely!" He looked at his watch. "The grocery downstairs has just opened. Let's go shopping Mademoiselle, shall we?" He led us out the door we had entered, down the stairs, through another metal door in the parking garage and into a long hallway, on the side of which were several other metal doors. "I own part of this city block," he explained, "and lease to several tenants. These doors allow me access if necessary, but the only one I use often is at the end of the hallway."

He had his own private entrance into the back of the grocery store. He opened it, and announced himself, "Bonjour!"

"Bonjour!" An unseen man's voice replied.

I had Monique by the hand. When we stepped into the back of the store my nose was assailed by the luscious fragrance of fresh baked goods.

It was a small, clean, up-scale urban grocery. The grocer was about the same age as our host.

"Bonjour Pol."

"Bonjour Monsieur Lecuyer. What can I help you with this morning?"

"We need eggs, bacon, and some potatoes for frying."

"Ah, I have just the type!"

Monique was standing in front of the glass case ogling the fresh baked goods.

"Marc, would it upset the character of your breakfast if we included some fresh croissants?"

"Croissants would compliment the big American breakfast quite well sir, especially with some of that red currant jelly."

The grocer was smiling. Monsieur Lecuyer was fun to shop with. He pondered. "Perhaps we should get supplies for dinner as well?"

I had an idea. "Do you like Indian-style curry? Céline could be easily persuaded into cooking later."

"Excellent idea!"

We carried our supplies up into the kitchen. I was pleased, because even working in an unfamiliar kitchen I was able to keep the hash browns crispy, and the slow-cooked eggs soft in the middle.

An old house cat made an appearance in the kitchen to eat, unwillingly capturing Monique's attention, who began chasing it in and out of the kitchen. I had to stop her. "Monique, don't chase the old cat. If you want to make friends with her, find what room she is in and calmly sit down on the floor on the other side of the room and wait. Be patient. If she wants to get to know you she will come over to meet you. Don't try to pick her up. She might bite and scratch. Okay?"

"Okay." She hurried off, leaving Monsieur Lecuyer and I alone at the dining room table with our coffee.

"Shall we continue our discussion from last night?" He asked.

"Yes, I would like that, thank you."

"The ideas that I will tell you I will summarize, because many statements can warrant entire discussions of their own. This morning, I would like to begin with the physical, social, and political reality of the life of Jesus, and how that leads to where we are sitting today. That leaves the spiritual, or occult side of the man and his family for another discussion. Actually, that discussion could not only fill a whole book, but an entire library of books." He paused to drink some coffee.

"First of all, his name in his time was Yeshua ben Joseph, of which 'Jesus' is a Latinized version. For accuracy, I prefer to refer to him as such. Did you know that Yeshua was of the royal line of David and heir to the throne of Israel?"

"No...not a carpenter?"

"No, but that leads to an important occult discussion, which we will set aside for another day."

"Alright, I'm listening."

"He was also a Rabbi. According to Hebrew law, one cannot become a Rabbi unless one is married. Yeshua was married to the woman known to us today as Mary of Bethany, also known as Mary Magdalene. While Yeshua was of the house of David, Mary was of the economically powerful house of Benjamin. The two houses had been at odds with one another for many years. In a nutshell, Mary was the princess, and Yeshua was the prince. Their union would create a potential king and queen of Israel. Can you perceive why that may have been threatening to the Romans?"

I thought about it. "Judea was under occupation by the Romans at the time. Israel had no king or queen."

"Exactly. In fact, the Hebrews were stirring up a lot of trouble for the Romans. The entire area was a hotbed for Jewish revolts and guerrilla attacks. It was costing Rome too much money garrisoning the area, but they were loath to give it up. When the Romans found out about the royal status of Yeshua and Mary, they issued an order to hunt them down and put them to the sword. That included the matriarchal side of the family, as well as Yeshua's brothers James and Thomas. It's as simple as that. The Romans kept immaculate records, some of which survive today. The order still exists."

"What actually happened to Yeshua deserves another discussion, but we know the basics of it because it's all been emphasized heavily by Christian churches of all types. What happened to Mary of Bethany is much less well known, because the Church of Rome has gone to great pains to cover it up. With the help of Joseph of Arimathea, she escaped to a Jewish community far from Judea in the south of France."

He paused to drink the last of his coffee. "Some accounts claim that Yeshua had sired two children with Mary, and others only one—a daughter. She's the important one because she had children who eventually married into the royal line of the Sicambrian Franks, which evolved into the kings and queens of the Merovingian dynasty. The Sicambrian Franks had their own related dynastic history which contributed to the power of the royal line. That leads to more scholarly discussions about the Franks' origins in Arcadia and Troy."

"Troy?" The *Iliad* and the *Odyssey* tales fascinated me.

"Yes. Consider the Trojan place names in France, like Troyes and Paris," he said before continuing, "Several hundred years before the apex of the Merovingian dynasty, a counsel of religious leaders assembled at the Council of Nicea in A.D. 325. You have probably heard of that."

"Yes, Constantine was in charge of the council."

"Well said actually, because Constantine totally controlled the outcome. Contrary to popular belief, Constantine was not a Christian. He was however, Emperor. What do you think is more important to any politician: religion or power?"

I didn't even have to think about that. "Power. They may use their religious leanings to curry the favor of the populace, but when it comes to push and shove..."

"Exactly," he cut in. "At the time, there was no bible yet as we know it. There were however, collections of writings and manuscripts that were held by different Christian sects that disagreed on some fundamental issues. Constantine could see the power of the Christians burgeoning, and wanted to maintain control of the movement. He knew that if there were, instead of one church with one doctrine, many different sects with opposing ideas, the controllable power would be diffused. Any rational mind will eventually begin to ask questions. If religious leaders cannot agree on any single doctrine, then someone must be right, while the others are wrong. The next rational question would be to wonder if perhaps they are all wrong!"

"I get it," I said.

"Every morning when the religious elders from all over the Mediterranean would enter the council chamber, they had to first walk between two long rows of soldiers who stood silently with their swords drawn. It was not even a thinly *veiled* threat. So Constantine had his way in solidifying a single doctrine. All other ideas were branded as heresy."

"So the Roman Catholic doctrine as we know it today

is an assembly of different ideas and writings that were chosen to be in a collection—the Bible— by men with a highly political agenda. Some may call it a religion, while others deem it more of a religious dynasty. Naturally the organization is threatened by anything that would tend to upset the dynasty."

"Constantine actually created the idea of heresy, which spread like a festering plague to eventually coalesce into the Spanish Inquisition. The idea still haunts us today. Before his time, many religions operated in the Roman social arena with few problems. One could pick and choose, like a smörgåsbord at a table."

"Constantine may have solidified the Church of Rome, but it was a step backwards in consciousness. That ushered in the 'Dark Ages', which were deemed 'dark' because Rome lost control of the lands taken by the Visigoths, the Sicambrian Franks, their progeny the Merovingians, and finally the Cathar society; all of which were less than aligned with the Roman Catholic doctrine. The fact that the Roman Empire dissolved and lost their technical prowess was a result of their own undoing. The Church of Rome however, persisted and flourished. It is almost as if an empire was sacrificed and displaced by a religious dynasty. It's not nearly that simplistic though."

"Your version of history does make sense."

"We must keep in mind that this is merely my personal interpretation. Another Priory member would probably relate their own ideas, but they are generally going to be in the same vein."

"So, you are leading up to the Merovingian dynasty?"

"Yes. The mystic kings of the Mérovée are a fascinating study: the stuff of legends. Whatever the truth of it all is, there is no question that they were the direct descendants of Yeshua and Mary."

"And that was threatening to the church?"

"Yes, but it was their entire society that was threatening. Let's paint a picture of two different societies; at least in their ideal forms. It's never so clear, but we will go to extremes to illustrate a point."

"Imagine this: The fundamental belief of one society is that every man, woman and child has the potential to be a divine being. Even the animals are considered to have evolving souls. That society believes that Yeshua was trying to remind us of that. The leaders of that society are admired by the people as strong leaders as well as highly spiritual men and women. The king or queen are not followers of, or subject to any religion. The royalty takes their job very seriously, and considers it a sacred task; one of guiding an entire society towards higher consciousness. The grail kings are the shepherds of Arcadia so to speak."

"Another society has been taught that every man, and particularly every woman are already sinners when they are born. They are threatened with following the rules of their religion to the letter or they may suffer dire consequences in the afterlife. Their rulers are coronated by their religious leaders, and so therefore are subject to them."

He raised his eyebrows. "So what would the psychological profile of the king of the first group be compared to the psychological profile of the king of the second group?"

"Well," I said. "I would enjoy drinking wine in the shade with the first king...and flee in the darkness of the night from the second!"

Monsieur Lecuyer laughed, "I do appreciate your sense of humor Marc."

"Some think I'm a sarcastic wise guy."

"I get it. *The Three Stooges*." He chuckled.

"I apologize for transgressing. We are discussing such lofty subjects."

"We would not be human without humor, which actually defines us. The two words do originate from the same root. You know, there is a cinema close by and... I must confess that since my wife is no longer with me there are a few evenings when I seek a reprieve from my alchemical studies. Lets just say that I am quite familiar with the three wise men from New Jersey. I hope you won't mention it to other Priory members."

"Oh, I wouldn't think of it."

"Somehow I know that I can trust you to keep a secret."

"My lips are sealed. So the tradition to coronate a king or queen began when?"

"Good question, and one extremely important development that has been overlooked by historians. Lawyers tend to see it more clearly." He continued, "The church plotted for over two hundred years to depose the Merovingian kings. That is how long their focus is—through generations of clergy. It was a difficult task, because the Merovingian kings—such as Clovis and Theodoric, were powerful. Finally, King Dagobert II was assassinated, which left control of the kingdom in the hands of the mayor of the palace, Pepin the Fat. He was not of the bloodline, and as planned, acquiesced control to the church. His great grandson was none other than Charlemagne, who became the first French king to be coronated by the Roman Catholic Church.

The church actually cooked up the idea of coronation. Before he became Emperor, Charlemagne was invited to a special mass in Rome. At some point in the ceremony, the Pope stepped up from behind him and placed a crown on his head—in full view of everyone. They were essentially establishing the idea that it was *they* who awarded the right for an individual to become king. For the first time, the church became king makers, and king deposers. Before that time, royalty was strictly inherited. Religious leaders had no say in the matter. Apparently Charlemagne was very uncomfortable with it. Since that time, non-bloodline rulers have tried to marry bloodline spouses to legitimize their positions—even to this day!"

"Separation of church and state." I mused.

"Yes, the Masonic writers of your superb American Constitution were well aware of the issue. The Priory influenced them."

"Really?"

"We will get to that later. Now—Dagobert II did have a young son, who escaped, allowing that part of the vine, or bloodline to continue. There are others."

"We will then jump forward several hundred years. The origins of the Prieuré de Sion go far back into prehistory and are associated with the ancient mystery schools. But the order was formally, secretly established prior to the first crusade. The first directive of the order was to fetch the documents, treasure, and artifacts that they knew were hidden under the Temple of Solomon in Jerusalem. The task was assigned to the nine original knights, mostly bloodline descendents, who later became commonly known as the Templars."

"Much has been written concerning the history of the

Templar order, but what is generally not known is that within the order there was a small group that explored more esoteric practices—like alchemy for example. The order within the order was directly connected to the Prieuré de Sion."

"From there, and from elsewhere popular tales and songs were written and disseminated. The Grail legends were created—The *Perlesvaus, Parzival, Gallahad, The Green Knight*, the Arthurian stories and others—all using Cathar and Merovingian symbolism and ideology. The idea was to educate and inspire the European community using a facet of the human psyche that no church, no despot, no bully can ever take away from the individual—imagination!"

Monsieur Lecuyer paused and produced a Mona Lisa smile. "You see, we are warriors of a different order. We once used to fight in the corporeal world, but now we challenge first ourselves, and then we strive to work for change in the world we live in—nonviolently."

Jacques! He read my mind, held up a finger, and said, "Lets go for a walk, shall we?"

His neighborhood was clean, orderly, with a mixture of homes, businesses, and light industry. We walked a good distance until we came to the river, where we found a park bench where we could talk and watch the motorboats and barges pass by. It was a lovely day, partially sunny, warm but brisk with a breeze.

Monsieur Lecuyer's position seemed to be one of overseeing and protecting the Favreau family. There were questions that I had harbored that had seemed to be too sensitive to bring up with Céline and the family.

"Could you tell me what happened to Céline's parents?"

"She never told you?"

"She's a very private person, and she's lost both her parents and her first husband."

"Before Germany attacked Poland in 1939, an element of the Ahnenerbe SS sent agents into European countries to locate and assassinate gentry of all kinds, bloodline or not. Since there were some leaks in information from the Teutonic Knights, as well as sharing from the Thule society, they were well aware of the Priory. The Nazi's were bent on world domination, and somehow considered the established gentry a potential unnecessary obstacle to their plans."

"The SS murdered Céline's parents?"

"Yes, right before the war began. Céline was sixteen."

We watched as a large luxury boat passed under the bridge.

He was thoughtful—reminiscing. "In the early years of this century, before the first war, the consciousness of societies worldwide was beginning to expand. Asia was beginning to open up, and freer from oppression, the western world began to wonder and explore ideas concerning the greater minds of men and women. The art and music that was produced from roughly about 1870 until the war in 1914 illustrates what people were becoming interested in. Magical and mystical themes were common: paintings depicting fairies or gods and goddesses, and composers such as our own Claude Debussy were also expressing those ideas."

"I noticed the paintings in your study."

"Yes, and there are more; my small mystical collection. Few of them have much value—prints from book illustrations and lesser artists. I just like them.

Those were the days of my youth."

He continued. "In those days, fortune telling, seances, and occult study groups were popular. Most of it was pure charlatanism, but nevertheless, it points to what flavor of ideas people were beginning to entertain." His eyes narrowed as he looked across the river at nothing. "Then they cooked up World War I to squelch it."

"What?"

"You probably don't realize that most of our recent wars were planned in advance and orchestrated deftly by those that represent huge financial interests." He turned, looked me and raised his eyebrows. "Even your American civil war was carefully manipulated."

"That's hard to believe. What about slavery?"

"Yes, now *that* is hard to believe—that in the 'land of the free' such a barbaric practice still persisted. What the power elite did was to use the emotionally charged slavery issue as a tool to divide the country into two halves and fight—then they simply collected the spoils. Classic Machiavellian technique."

"What spoils?"

"This is a subject we could discuss all afternoon. I would prefer not to become side-tracked with it. But consider this: Before the civil war the American government operated reasonably well using their own currency backed by gold. After the war America began using a different currency controlled by the European banking elite. Ever since 1865 the American people have been in debt."

"What do you mean?" I asked defensively.

"I believe it's generally referred to as the 'national debt'. As an American citizen, did you ever think to ask the question: To whom are we in debt to? And why?"

"As I said I would really like to stop here."

I wasn't satisfied. "But what about World War II? Hitler was a maniac!"

"Of course, but lunatics like Hitler are merely pieces on a chessboard. On the same board were also Mussolini, Stalin, Churchill, Hirohito, Roosevelt and Hoover. But it's not chess. No matter who wins the game the players profit. The important thing to remember is that it is in their best interest to keep a populace subtly enslaved by keeping them in a survival mode: working, consuming, and barely getting by—but not thinking! A war serves quite well for that."

He paused and sighed. "The whole idea of a free country in the new world was dreamed up by the Priory long before the American revolution. It is the most important project the Priory has undertaken in centuries, and has been largely successful." He grinned at me and laid his palm out flat. "The Statue of Liberty? Our gift!"

I got it. As unorthodox as it all was, it did make sense.

"Did you fight in the Great War sir?"

"Oh yes, I was in the Seaforth Highlander regiment."

"A Scottish regiment?"

"Its too much to explain now. We have always been allied with the Scots."

"Didn't the highlanders have to wear kilts into battle?"

"Oh yes, we wore kilts. The highland regiments were valorous and fought with great passion." He smirked proudly as he reminisced. "The Germans, with little affection but a measure of respect dubbed the highlanders: 'The ladies from hell'."

He was promoting non-violence and yet he was once a soldier like I was, but in an even uglier war, with fixed bayonets in pitched battle.

We tend to try to believe in a dualistic black and white world: a world where there is good and evil, right and wrong—but it is simply never that clear. It is far more complicated than that. Where would right be without wrong? If evil were finally banished forever, then good would be forced into involuntary retirement. They are two sides of the same coin; dependent on each other. I perceived that Olivier's *modus operandi* was actually the evolution of his soul from lifetime to lifetime. But he would occasionally indulge in a silly movie just for fun. He was disciplined but was neither rigid or inflexible. I saw it as a admirable model to follow. We create art and music, we love and we dance. But still we are human. We smell, we defecate and we kill and consume other animals and life forms. We can struggle to deny it, but the effort is futile. It is our undeniable reality here, and the drama is *not* in black and white; It's a grand production in full living color.

A benign gust of wind buffeted us from the south, as we paused to observe the bustle in slow-motion on the river. I relaxed into the goose-bump breeze. I respected the wind, and had formed a kind of armistice with it. It was in fact a furtive, powerful wind that had brought me here, where my life had changed so dramatically.

I looked over at him. "Tell me about Jacques."

Olivier clasped his fingers together on his crossed legs, and took in a breath before letting it out quickly. "Jacques has had a very difficult adult life. As a young man he joined the French army only to see most of his comrades die ugly, painful deaths, and his country surrender in humiliation. He became a formidable member of the resistance."

"When the war ended he continued to fight. That is all he knows. He is obsessed with it." He rubbed his forehead. "As I mentioned before, as Priory members we endeavor to fight our battles without aggression. It has been a policy since the inception of the Prieuré de Sion. We do not follow the tenet of 'an eye for an eye'."

He looked at me with his head tilted down through his eyebrows. "Jacques does not follow the rules." He let that sink in. "Jacques is a tiger. A hunter of the hunters. In the resistance he became a superb operative with a formidable intuitive sense; and is a practitioner of Jujitsu and kick boxing. He is set on a personal crusade; a vendetta to eliminate those that killed his best friend. That is why I keep him close. Otherwise he would be a completely rogue element. At least this way I can maintain a modicum of control."

He shook his head. "Recently he caught up with one of his 'enemies' in Italy that he has been at odds with for years. Jacques tortured him in an effort to extract information, but the man had taken poison when Jacques caught him. He was an important operative, and Jacques feels that the murder of his father is in direct retribution." He looked thoughtful. "I am not so sure. We have more to discuss this afternoon with Céline."

"How did Jacques ever find the time to learn Jujitsu and kick boxing?"

"They studied the martial arts before the war. That is where they met Jean."

"You mean Céline studied Jujitsu as well?"

"Why yes...You didn't know?"

I shook my head. "You learn something every day!"

"I hope you have learned more than that today.

There is much more to come you know!"

"I didn't mean it that way sir. It's just an American expression. It means a lot to me that you are spending your time to teach me. Xavier taught me many things as well."

"My late wife and I could not have children, for what reason we never knew. Jacques has been a kind of son for me—my wayward son."

We both left it unsaid, but the respect and affection between us was culturing. I, who had never had a father, was hungry for paternal influence, and accepted Oliviers guidance; just as I had welcomed Xavier's love as a surrogate parent.

We strolled back through the bustling streets of the old city of Lyon to the keep of Monsieur Olivier Lecuyer; the shield bearer for the Favreau family, and as I was soon to learn—the Rémillards as well.

15

The End of Innocence

When we returned Jacques had arrived, and he and Céline were drinking coffee and talking in the dining room. She had spoken with Camille on the telephone. When we looked at each other we both knew what the other was thinking. I shook my head up and down in resignation.

She put her hand on my arm. "I'll tell her," she said.

We all went into the parlor, where Jacques took the position by the window.

Céline knelt down in front of Monique and told her about Xavier, making sure to reiterate that she had been correct in warning us. I knew what Céline was doing. She didn't want her daughter to shut down what appeared to be a remarkable sense of foresight, due to stress. If she associated that ability with Xavier's death she may habitually avoid it. It was a talent well worth nurturing.

It was one of the hardest things I had ever done; sitting on the edge of the chair watching the tears come to the eyes of my little fairy girl. It was the end of innocence.

I feared she would be processing it for days, weeks, years—scarred forever, and there was nothing I could do about it.

Jacques had paused between cigarettes to observe. He had been surprisingly gentle with his young niece. His jaw set in a grim line before he turned to look out the window and light up again. God help whoever got in Jacques way now.

It was then that a tiny miracle occurred. The old cat that Monique had been unsuccessfully chasing around the house all day came into the room, stopped and looked around. Who knows what cats see with their eyes? She jumped up on the sofa next to Monique, lay down with her back up against the girl and began to clean herself with her tongue. Monique reached out with a tenuous hand and touched her lightly. The cat feigned to ignore her. We all saw it happen, and watched in silence.

Monsieur Lecuyer left the room and returned a few minutes later with a tray full of lemonade and tall glasses.

As he was settling himself in a chair he began. "Marc. When Céline became pregnant with Monique, Camille called me and told me about you. One never knows, but she was fairly sure you intended to return to France. I took the liberty to investigate your background. I hope you are not too sensitive about this. I had to. It is part of my duties. American soldiers are numerous and princesses are rare, no?" He raised his eyebrows.

"I understand sir."

Monique, her eyes still red leaned up against Céline and listened, with one hand on the cat.

"Your mother, Armelle Rémillard was born in upstate New York, where she spent the first few years of her life before they moved to Montreal. Its seems there was family there. Her family tree bore enough interesting genealogy to goad me into continuing further than I needed to. I traced the vine all the way back to the first group of settlers in Canada, at least in our modern era."

He took a sip of lemonade. "In 1390 a Scottish nobleman by the name of Henry Sinclair built a small settlement in what is now called Nova Scotia."

"1390? That's a century before Columbus," I said.

"Marc...Columbus did not discover America. Someday we can talk all about that."

"Alright."

"There Henry Sinclair secretly housed a group of bloodline refugees. They abandoned the stockade-type refuge a few years later when there began to be too much traffic off of the coast for their liking. From there they moved to an island in the middle of the river to form what is now called Montreal. That group formed the original heart of the city."

"Wait. Are you saying that my mother was bloodline?"

"Quite, and your father was as well." He drank some more lemonade. "Your father's name was Nicolas Corbenic. His great-grandfather was the Marquis de Corbenic who, as a young man fled from France during the revolution. Your given name, 'Marc' is actually an affectation of your title."

"Title?"

"Why yes, you are the Marquis de Corbenic, and Céline is the Marquise," he said with smug satisfaction.

"You must be kidding me."

"No, I am quite serious."

I looked at Céline, who shrugged her shoulders.

This was the first time she had heard this as well.

"Forgive me for my ignorance, but *what* pray tell is a marquis?"

"It's a hereditary title slightly higher in rank than a count, but less than a duke. In the olden days, a marquis controlled the marche, or the border lands, which made it a tougher responsibility than a count's job, who managed the safer 'county' lands in the interior of a kingdom."

"So what good is that now?"

"We have little cause to use our titles these days. It would only come up if—say you were attending a formal state dinner with the King of Denmark. You would be introduced as Marc Rémillard, Marquis de Corbenic, and Céline Rémillard, Marquise de Corbenic. That is of course assuming that you continue to use your mother's maiden name as your surname." He mused. "That does become confusing."

"Well, I'll have to check my calender, but since I have not received any invitations from the King of Denmark lately it's probably not going to come up—right!"

He laughed and pointed his finger. "One never knows! The important thing is that you two found each other. How that works in the fabric of our world remains a mystery. Its like when you run into someone you know in a foreign place. The mathematical odds such meetings will occur are almost nonexistent, but the fact is, it happens all the time. You see? There are threads that run through our cosmos that connect us in ways we generally can't see. Do you know how much the two of you look alike? You could be mistaken for brother and sister. Your frequencies are that similar!"

He swirled the ice around in his glass.

"So I did not receive my fathers name. I have been aware of that for some time now."

"Yes." He tapped at his head. "This is what Sherlock Holmes has deduced. Your father did die mysteriously. One way or another your mother fled. They had only been married for a short time, and she was pregnant with you. Since she was born in the U.S.A., she was an American citizen, and probably went through the border into the U.S.A. using her passport that was issued in her maiden name."

"That makes sense."

"She took you into hiding in a remote corner of the country."

"The house is in a trust within a trust within a trust..."

"Of course, that is how we set up financial structures. But I have something to tell you." He paused. "I do not think your mothers death was an accident."

"An auto accident." I automatically repeated.

"Did she know how to drive?"

"No."

"Then how was it that she died in a car alone?"

He let me think about that for a moment.

"Why would they go after her now?" I finally asked.

"That is a piece of the puzzle I am trying to figure out. She was only forty-two. She was possibly still capable of bearing children."

"My mother?"

"*Yes* Marc. That is an only child talking. They are always after the women of child-bearing age. Céline is a prime target."

Monique was still listening.

"It still just doesn't make sense!" He exclaimed. "Like

you said. Why now? Because she was on a twenty year-old hit list?" He cradled his chin with his thumb and a knuckle. "Something happened."

Jacques spoke up. "I heard you killed an SS officer Marc."

Monique's eyes were wide. I didn't necessarily want her to hear this. They all waited for an answer.

I nodded my head.

Jacques was thinking. "As a paratrooper, what was your mission involved with?"

"They never told us. It was unusual. There were OSS officers on our two planes."

"I wonder what they were up to?" He said. "Right before that, the SS had plundered some estates, and had taken some important documents we were looking for."

"The resistance?"

"We were under a directive from the Priory."

Monsieur Lecuyer added, "The Priory was an instrumental force behind the resistance. Why are you asking Jacques?"

"It just came into my head."

"At the time, the SS was grabbing everything they thought might be important or valuable, including French gold." The gentleman looked at me. "Marc, I must be frank. When I investigated your mother's background, I found that she was living on very limited finances. Is there something you are not telling us? Were the officers carrying any documents or gold with them?"

I skirted the question. "That is what the OSS Major in Paris asked me. At least about any documents."

"OSS Major?" Jacques asked.

I was still trying to slip out of it. "They sent me back to headquarters in Paris because I...removed an SS Standartenfuhrer from...active duty."

"Yeah, with a Tommy-gun wasn't it?"

Thanks Jacques! "Anything that involved the SS the OSS wanted to know about," I added.

All of a sudden Céline turned, looked at me and spoke with certainty, "The strong box! It had gold in it!" *The darn woman was psychic.*

Monsieur Lecuyer arrested the situation. "Wait!" He held his hand up. "Marc, if you did in fact secure some French gold, we—the Priory are glad you did. If you, as Céline's husband had not already been wealthy we would have made sure that—through investments, you were comfortable. She is very important. I must also add that the very idea of the Swiss bank as it exists to-day was originally initiated by Priory members. It is no accident that they first appeared in business directly prior to the Revolution." He paused to press his point. "As an American I don't expect you to really understand this but we represent *old* wealth. We are not at all con-cerned with the gold. What we are trying to locate are any ancient documents. I am not at liberty to tell you why. I am sorry."

"Ancient?" For the first time in five years I remembered that tin case, "I forgot all about it." I admitted. "When the OSS officer questioned me I thought he was talking about modern documents. I gave him the orders that I had found on the SS officer." I looked up sheepishly. "There was a document written in...I think...Latin, on parchment. It was wrapped in leather in a metal case."

Too calmly, the gentleman inquired, "Do you, by

chance know where it is now?"

My face flushed and turned red. I felt like a total fool. "It's behind a board in the wall at the l'ermitage ancienne."

Monsieur Lecuyer sat back in his chair. "Good. Well, it looks like you and Jacques have a little job to do!"

Jacques wasn't finished. "What did you tell the OSS officer in Paris?"

"As little as I could."

"But you gave him the orders that were written in German?"

"Yes."

"Can you read German?"

"Not really."

"So they may have mentioned the movement of a document." He held a finger up. "I'll bet that's how the Vatican found out. That's the connection!"

I shook my head. I didn't know what he was talking about.

"It does make sense," Monsieur Lecuyer said.

Jacques was looking at me as if I were an idiot.

"Jacques." The gentleman scolded. "Marc, do you remember that I told you earlier that intelligence agencies share information? The Vatican and the CIA are reluctant bed partners."

"Yeah—the *homo's*."

"Jacques," he said under his breath.

There is a little girl present.

It was my turn to break it up. "What you are suggesting is that I may be inadvertently responsible for the death of my own mother, as well as..." I looked at Jacques. "Xavier?"

Monsieur Lecuyer was diplomatic. "We may never

know for certain. But right now we can act, and retrieve that document." He stopped and pondered. "Then there's the Raoul connection to consider. They may have gotten information from two sides. That would give them enough to act."

Jacques was nodding his head in a 'yes'. "It's not you're fault Marc. They just keep crawling out of the sewer—like rats!"

If that was conciliatory, I accepted.

The session ended. Monique was overloaded, so I took her into the bedroom and put her on the bed for a nap.

"Papa. Did you really kill someone?"

I sighed. "You're a big girl now aren't you?"

She nodded.

"I wish our world were a fairy tale place. It is gradually getting better. We are working on that, but I think we might need your help. Okay?"

She nodded again.

"When you wake up your mom will be cooking a curry."

I kissed her on the forehead and closed the door.

16

Warriors of a Different Order

The next morning I waited for Jacques to arrive from where ever it was he slept. Where his place was and what it looked like I didn't want to know, and I doubt anyone was allowed to anyway.

I drove. He directed me out of Lyon. We didn't talk much. We were like two male cats that were forced to live in the same household. He chained-smoked the entire way, lighting one cigarette with what was left of the previous one.

Jacques did question me about the car. He was concerned that we would be recognized in the neighborhood by operatives. Even though I told him how I had gotten the car only the day before we left he was still uncomfortable about it.

At one point he blurted out, "I don't know why it should take two of us to get a *document* anyway!"

I got it. He was not a salad-eater—a retriever of documents. Jacques was a carnivore—a man hunter. He was hungry, and this assignment was keeping him from his food.

We approached the l'ermitage ancienne the back way, via the mountain road.

The document case wasn't there. I couldn't believe it, and searched the whole cottage. It was gone. More than frustrated, I went outside where Jacques was leaning up against the car.

"They got the document didn't they?" He took another drag—thinking. "That's what they were after."

"I'd like to check on my house. Do you think it's safe?"

"Probably, we'd better do it quickly. We don't want anyone to see us."

The was no car at the house. The door wasn't locked. We went in, looked around and went up into the kitchen. There was food on the counter that I didn't recognize. Jacques and I had both failed to have our weapons out.

A man appeared in the hallway with a pistol pointed at me. He couldn't see Jacques, who was in front of the refrigerator. When the assailant moved forward Jacques pushed his pistol hand aside and with the lower part of his right leg launched a swift powerful front kick into the man's knee, buckling it backwards. At the same time the assassin's free fist struck out and contacted Jacques jaw, which pushed him backwards, before the assassin crumpled onto the floor with a crushed knee. The pistol slid across the floor.

I reached for my pistol, but realized there was another man in the hallway with a gun trained on me. He looked back and forth from me to Jacques, deciding who to shoot. *He has a directive to kill only bloodline members.*

Suddenly, he somehow lurched forward—his chin on his chest. Jacques right foot reached out with his whole leg in a long upward kick, slamming the top of his shoe squarely into the man's down-turned face. The assailants head jerked backwards before contacting the sink cabinet. He was out cold.

Jacques already had his own pistol trained on the man with the broken knee, who was panting, with sweat seeping out of his face. He had red hair.

In spite of the harsh reality of my discovery of Xavier, up until that time the persecutors had been anonymous: faceless foes. But here they were, two of them in my home—flesh and blood, with a twisted, murderous ill intent.

I saw red.

"Who sent you here?" I yelled. The red-haired fanatic offered no response, just a defiant, wooden glare.

I slowly, determinedly stood straight up, reached into my wallet pocket and pulled out the Walther PP, grabbed the man's collar with my left hand and pressed the barrel of the pistol into his forehead.

"Your ilk murdered my mother! You have killed and threaten to kill my family in *my home*!" A rage of fury surged through my veins like the hot orange fire of a forge, flowing out of my eyes as they watered up in a lame attempt to cool it.

A deep fear entered the zealot's eyes as he tried to melt into the wall behind him. The devil incarnate was boring a hole into his forehead with a pistol barrel, and into his soul with those flaming eyes.

My finger tightened on the trigger. I thought of my noble mother silently struggling all of those years. I thought of Xavier—that beautiful man. I thought of Monique, the tears coming to her eyes. I could feel the final resistance of the trigger as I involuntarily squeezed it like a boa constrictor tightening on its prey.

I closed my eyes.

We are warriors of a different order.

"Marc...Calm down...You're scaring me."

I'm scaring Jacques?

"Who's this guy?"

Jacques had his pistol pointed down the hallway.

It was Father Bouchet, with a broom in his hand.

A weapon.

"It's alright Jacques. He's my friend."

Jacques looked at the priest as if he were from another planet.

It was Father Bouchet who had pushed the second assassin forward into the kitchen by jamming the end of the broom handle into the back of his head. He looked down at the broom as if it were a bloody spear.

"Stay alert," Jacques said. "They probably have other weapons."

He was right. We found knives and a pocket derringer with a silencer attached to it. It was professionally machined and flawlessly melted into the body of the tiny pistol. Between the two of us, Jacques was the calm one.

"What do we do with them?" I asked.

Father Bouchet was still standing, planted in the hallway. "We must report this to the police!" He said.

"No, no, and no," said Jacques. "By nightfall of the next day they will be free. The police receive a phone call, and then they let them go. It happens every time. They return, and then I have to fight them *again!*"

"But..."

Jacques cut him off. "Look *priest,* you're way over your head here." He moved closer into the hallway until they

158

were face to face. "Besides, what are you going to tell them? That a man of God such as yourself bludgeoned some guy with a broom handle?" Jacques' anger was deep seated. He kept taunting in a sarcastic tone. "You used a weapon. Isn't your God much more important than your friend?"

Father Bouchet was passive but defiant as they stared each other down. He broke the stare by looking at me.

"Marc is my friend," he said quietly.

Almost imperceptibly, Jacques nodded his head up and down as he held Robert's gaze. "Perhaps there is hope after all." He turned and went back into the kitchen.

I looked at Father Bouchet. "What did happen Robert?"

"I came to check on the house, and found the door open. I came upstairs and noticed fresh food on the counter. I heard someone entering downstairs and hid in the broom closet. I've been in there all afternoon."

"I'll remember that technique." Jacques said under his breath.

"Back down Jacques, he helped us. So what do you usually do with them?"

Jacques began his sentence much too calmly. "Oh, I usually just...sacrifice them TO THE DEVIL!" He screamed into the assassin's face.

The guy didn't even flinch. He was far more afraid of me. Jacques may have been threatening, but I *was* the devil. Every time he looked at me his eyes had the perpetually fearful eyes of a sheep.

"Perhaps you shouldn't mention to anyone that this happened Robert." I said.

"Oh right...He will do it in confession." Jacques snorted.

"I know about the Prieuré de Sion," Robert said. "Is that why Xavier was murdered?"

"Yes." *The man on the floor is listening.*

"Are you going to kill these men?" Robert asked.

"I will not kill them. I promise." *I can't speak for Jacques.*

"You know where the key is. Can you look after the place for us?"

Father Bouchet nodded, turned and left. I wondered if I would ever see him again. If the man with the crumbled knee lived, they would probably have to deal with Father Robert Bouchet eventually.

We tied the men up, and put them in the car. Jacques insisted on driving. On the road in front of the l'ermitage ancienne he stopped the car. He didn't look at me.

"Get out Marc. I will be back in awhile."

I hesitated, then threw open the door, got out and watched him zoom away. At first I felt sick to my stomach. It became incredibly quiet. The same birds were singing high in the trees as they had been a few days before. I went back and sat on the stone bench, and forced myself to drink some of the water. By the time Jacques returned I was calm in a numb kind of a way.

"Shall we go?" I asked.

He shrugged his shoulders. I let him drive. I didn't mention the assassins, and we never discussed it afterwards. As we were approaching Lyon, I remembered there was something I needed to ask him.

"You and Jean were best friends Jacques," I said. "What happened to him?"

"They got him."

"The same group do you think?"

"Probably." He was speaking to me more civilly now, almost normally.

"We were both in the army together in 1940 when a German offensive began to drive the French forces hard back towards Paris. Their tanks and ground attack planes were cutting us to pieces. We were not fools, and could see that we were fighting a loosing battle. We deserted, and fled into the mountains together. We were not cowards—we just wanted to live to fight another day. Three days later the French forces surrendered."

"Jean and I were instrumental in forming a cornerstone of the resistance. The Germans knew about both of us and actively pursued us."

He took another long, nervous drag off of his cigarette. "I think that since Italy and Germany were allies, intelligence information was shared between them, and the fanatics got a hold of some of it. Besides, even if the Nazi's didn't care for a group of operatives they were always more than willing to let them do their dirty work for them. This group we are dealing with has proven to have friends in high places. They can really pull some strings when they need to."

He looked over at me. "You know you're never going to be able to live there again."

I didn't say anything.

"You built that house didn't you?"

I nodded.

"Nice place. I'd be glad to help you retrieve some of your things. We'd have to do it carefully."

I couldn't believe it. He was actually being nice.

"Thanks Jacques. I could really use some expert help. So you were telling me about Jean."

"It was definitely not the Nazi's that got them. It was the same style as...with my father—small caliber bullet to the head."

"Them?"

"He was with a woman that bore a resemblance to Céline. They killed her as well. They were actually after Céline of course. Even though the SS was after him, Jean would not have been important to the fanatics. Afterwards, Céline thought that Jean had been unfaithful to her."

"Oh...I get it now. Well...was he?"

"I was his best friend, and I don't even know. It's not really important now is it?"

"She's still tight-lipped about it," I said.

"I think the reason that Céline has been safe for the last eight years is that the crazies think they already got her when they took Jean out."

"That's one more mystery that's been cleared up."

When we returned to Lyon, Monsieur Lecuyer's disappointment in our failure to retrieve the document was eclipsed by his distress that we had encountered and disposed of two agents. He was upset, and I felt that I had failed him. Jacques didn't seem to care. He just went to the window, sat down and lit another cigarette. Olivier looked at me. He had expected better of me.

"With all respects sir, what was I supposed to do? Try to tell Jacques what to do with the very men that killed his father? The .22 caliber derringer we found on them was probably the murder weapon. Besides, once we had captured them, they learned Jacques' face and status, had identified me and our car, and gathered other information as well. And Father Bouchet! He would have to be eliminated."

"He's right Olivier." Jacques added, then pulled the derringer out of his pocket and handed it up to him.

Monsieur Lecuyer looked down at the polished artifice of death in his hand. "What does one do with such ignorant hate?" He mused. Then he turned, took a deep breath and let it out in exasperation. "Now I have two warriors to look after."

I felt chagrined. "You told me that the grail king's sacred duty was to guide and protect the people. Weren't there times when he would have to defend his borders against aggression?"

"An unpleasant reality of our world." He looked over at Jacques, and then back at me. "You were, in fact protecting others." He conceded. Once again he looked over at Jacques, and then back at me. "I am glad you both returned safe," he said curtly.

Olivier disappeared for several hours after that. Whatever he did down there in his workshop, he was in a more normal mood when he appeared again for dinner.

17

The Wine of Our Ancestors

After dinner, Monsieur Lecuyer offered us glasses of a dark red wine.

"This is a powerful wine," I remarked

"It is from just south of here. The grapevines are grown on the steep slopes above the Rhône river."

"I like it. It has a lot of character," I commented

"It's one of my favorites, with an interesting history as well." He looked at Céline and asked, "Céline, have you heard the tale of 'The Wine of Our Ancestors'?"

She thought about it. "Not that I recall."

"Would you like to?"

"Yes, of course."

We settled in with Monique in between us, who was accustomed to hearing a story at bedtime. I cannot remember the last time I had been the recipient of a bedtime story, but somehow I remembered the protocol—listen, but questions may be asked. The dress code—pajama's. Neither Céline or I had our pajama's on but we relaxed into it anyway.

When Mary Magdalene landed in Provence fleeing from the Roman sword, she brought with her almost no possessions. She did bear an important secret though; one that only Jewish royalty were privy to.

When the boat with the three Marys in it floundered off of the southern coast near Saint Marie-de-la-Mère, a Gypsy matriarch waded out and pulled it into shore. The older woman apparently had foresight of their arrival. In fact, it was the Gypsies that sheltered the group temporarily until they established themselves with the Jewish community in southern France.

Mary, like her husband Yeshua, was an initiate of the Great Work in her own right. Before they were married, she studied with various masters much like he had. Mary had a gift for prophecy, but could also heal—like Yeshua could. She was more secretive however, choosing to hold her power close.

But Mary, like any woman, missed her husband, her homeland and yearned for the things she was familiar with.

At that time one of the most coveted wines in the middle east was made in Shiraz, near the Persian Gulf. It was expensive, particularly for those living in Judea, because it had to be hauled on camel back or shipped over two thousand kilometers on long, perilous journeys from Shiraz.

The royal couple however, had been quite wealthy, and drank the wine from Persia regularly.

It was possibly the same wine that was poured at the Last Supper, and certainly what was served at their wedding—the very same wedding in Cana when Jesus turned water into wine. You know—that story is not allegory or fable. He actually did that. What one person considers a miracle or "magic", another may view as ordinary. This telephone for example, would be thought of as magical a mere two hundred years ago.

So when Mary moved to France not only did she move away from the land she knew, she also lost access to the quality wines she was accustomed to drinking. Mary remembered the wine served at their wedding with fondness and respect, and the majesty of that wine grew as she told her children, and eventually her grandchildren about it during their bedtime stories.

Over a thousand years passed. During all of that time, Mary's important secret had been carefully passed from generation to generation inside the bloodline families. The secret was this: A vast treasure and important documents had been buried under the Temple of Solomon in Jerusalem prior to its destruction by the Romans. How that treasure was eventually wrestled from the bowels of the Temple is a tale for another night.

But from that we know that the bloodline families could keep a secret, and they also passed other stories down in the oral tradition.

Well—after the bedtime story of the wine had

been repeated over and over for a thousand years, the magical qualities of the wine gradually became grander and grander. It was like a fish story, where the fish becomes larger every time the story is told. It slowly transmuted into the best wine the world has ever known: The wine made from the vines the Nephilim brought from their far-away planet. The wine of Noah, made from the cuttings he saved and planted after the deluge. The wine of Mary and Jesus. The wine of our ancestors.

It came to pass that sometime during the third crusade there was a lady of the vine—a wealthy lady who had lost her husband and was bored with most of the typical preoccupations of life. She had reached middle age, and was not particularly attractive, but due to her wealth, there had been a few suitors. She was not interested. Husbands were difficult and demanding. She was perfectly happy in her home tended by her servants. Now this was when the Cathar society in the south was flourishing. The Cathars, with their passion for life, unknowingly created the loving, vibrant heart of France, which still beats steadily today.

The lady was a patron of the troubadours, so her home was often filled with music, the tales of the bards, dance, and laughter. She had carved out a small window in time in which to wonder, and to dream. One thing that captured her imagination was that old tale of the fabulous mystical, magical wine of Shiraz. She thought about it daily.

She could even see it in her chalice, and imagined it filling her soul with the spiritual essence of the Grail itself.

The lady lived in a grand home that looked out onto the Rhône river, not far south from here. The hillsides above the river rose up steeply, until they melted into the plains on one side, and the mountains on the other. It was precisely where the soldiers had assembled to embark on the Second Crusade, waiting to move up over the mountain pass together. As a little girl she remembered all of those gallant young men on horses, waiting for the arrival of the beautiful Eleanor, Queen of France, who was to accompany them on the crusade.

Many years had passed since then, but when the Third Crusade began the lady saw it as an opportunity. Even though it was extravagantly expensive, she decided to hire a crusader knight to procure some of the grapevines from Shiraz and bring them to her. She planned to plant them (or have them planted by others) and make (or have made) the sacred wine for herself.

The knight she chose was a mature crusader. He had already served as a young page boy during the disastrous second crusade. He was wise and knew his way around the holy land. He was to be paid well. As a knight, his professional career had not been particularly successful, and had rendered him with few resources. His title was: The Chevalier Henri Gaspard de Sterimberg, and his task was to bring cuttings of grapevines over twelve thousand kilometers from Shiraz to the comfortable home of our lady.

Henri had many adventures in the holy land endeavoring to procure the magical cuttings from far away Shiraz. As a Christian knight he would not have survived the journey deep into Persian territory, where the ancient southern Sumerian city of Shiraz lay. He chose instead to hire a Persian trader, who by both land and sea, would secure and import the cuttings to where the knight waited on the Island of Cyprus.

One particular Muslim trader was recommended by the Templars, who had their base on the island. For whatever reason that was never determined, the trader failed to return. Perhaps the unfortunate trader's ship sank in a storm or he was captured by pirates. The knight was then forced to hire yet another trader, and wait another year for the next season because grapevines will only produce viable cuttings during their dormant season in the winter.

Our knight came close to running out of money, so resorted to hiring out as a mercenary while he waited for the cuttings to arrive. When they finally did arrive, he sold his horse and armor to secure passage on a ship destined, amongst other stops, for the port of Marseilles. On the last leg of the journey, their ship was attacked by an Egyptian navy vessel. Fortunately, the Genoese captain was crafty, and his ship was more maneuverable than the larger

Egyptian galley. They managed to escape, but not before our knight had received an arrow to the leg. The crew held him down and dug the iron arrow point out of his leg and cauterized the wound. By the time they dumped him off in Marseilles he could barely walk.

In those days, commercial cargo was hauled up the Rhône river by a system of barges pulled against the current by oxen alongside the bank. A clear pathway was dedicated for the beasts, who were hitched to the barges with long, heavy ropes. With the last of his funds, the knight hired the longshoremen to haul the cuttings up-river, along with their other cargo. He hobbled alongside, unable to ride, but unwilling to let the cuttings out of his sight.

When he finally arrived he was exhausted, much of the last of his life energy spent.

The lady was glad to have her cuttings, but was not as appreciative as she could have been. It had been five full years since he had set out, and she felt it had taken him too long. It would be unfair to judge the lady too harshly. Having never traveled, she had no concept of how far he had gone, and having never had to labor for anything in her life, she could not understand the travails the man had been through.

He could travel no further, so she gave him a little hut up on the hillside to live in, and made sure he was taken care of for the remaining years of his life. He had experienced enough of the world, and chose to live out the rest of his days alone like a hermit; praying to his god and watching the last few seasons roll by.

After the long, hot, dry journey, few of the cuttings survived; not nearly enough to produce the grapes necessary to fill a barrel with wine. The local vigneron entrusted with the project waited for three years, took cuttings from the survivors and planted those. By the time they finally made the wine, and waited for it to age for a year, fourteen years had passed since the chevalier had begun his journey. He had passed away several years before, and the lady had gone from middle to old age. When they finally poured the finished wine into her cup she closed her eyes in a prayer before lifting the magical elixir to her lips.

She drank one sip. It was the only swallow she ever took of it. She wanted to like it, but couldn't bring herself to. She was accustomed to drinking the supple wines made by the Cistercian monks in the south. She didn't say anything. Women have pride just as men do. No one likes to admit to loosing a battle. Her displeasure however, was obvious to her servants.

Eventually the vines themselves heard, through the grumbling of the vigneron, that the lady was displeased with the grapes they had so lovingly produced on those difficult, steep, granite slopes.

So they changed, adapted to the soil and strengthened their trunks against the brutal mistral winter winds, and grew more vigorously to provide shelter from the blistering heat of summer. Yes, they altered their genetics to serve those that derived pleasure from them. Nature is pleased when all are happy.

Several generations later, they had worked out how to grow and make a good wine from the dark, thick-skinned grapes. The name of the lady has been long forgotten by history, but several hundred years later the villagers built a little stone chapel in honor of the hermit-knight up on the hillside amongst the vines where he had lived out the last of his days.

Today, the chapel is still nestled there, looking out towards the ever-flowing river. The wine produced from that vineyard is called Hermitage, and made from the Syrah grape. For better or for worse, it is the wine of our ancestors.

When we finally went to bed that night I was exhausted, but I still couldn't sleep. I kept thinking about the two men Jacques had driven off with. Even though they had wanted to murder my child, my wife, and myself—and had probably killed Xavier; I still felt responsible for them. I also kept thinking about Xavier. It was difficult to reconcile. I got up and tried to read, but I was too tired to read. It wasn't until the sun began to make it's presence known that sleep—the angel of compassion, managed to lay her gossamer blankets over me.

The room is made of plain unadorned stone, with an opening on one wall, and another on the opposite wall. Resting on the stone floor near one of the doorways is the tip of a moist, dusty black tail. The shape of the tip is unusual, vaguely resembling a fleur-de-lis. The tail curves into an adjoining room, only to disappear into another opening.

Looking back at the empty doorway, I know with certainty that is not my way. My path is towards the heart of the dragon.

There are many openings and hallways, but I follow the tail as it grows in breadth. Avoiding its touch, I press through the last opening and step into a huge, dark room. The tail meanders off into the blackness to the right.

The dragon is the key to my ascension—but I fear it.

A coward, I avoid the beast, and choose to instead explore much of the vast, ancient room. Columns, tombs, altars, and more—fading into the darkness. It is an underground temple.

There is time. She has infinite patience.

The dragon waits in the heart of the labyrinth.

18

The Quest

Céline arose earlier than usual. When I saw her I knew something was different. It took me a minute to place it because I had seen her that way only once before.

Céline had a vision.

We were at the table. "Did you...have an experience last night?"

She nodded her head in a yes.

"I think I will tell someone about it." She wasn't sure who.

"Do you want to call Camille?"

"I think I want to talk to Olivier."

"Shall I get him?"

She nodded her head. I brought her a cup of tea then went hunting for Monsieur Lecuyer in his house. He wasn't in his rooms. I found a stairwell that went down further than ground floor level. I knocked on the door at the bottom of the stairwell and called his name. Bustling sounds came from the other side of the door before he opened it.

There was what looked like a chemistry laboratory behind him.

"I am sorry to bother you sir but... Céline."

"What is it?"

"She has had a vision, and she has chosen you to relate it to. This doesn't happen very often."

"I know," he said as he shut the door and began to move into the hallway.

I left her alone with Olivier in the dining room, but she motioned for me to stay.

When we sat down I had an idea. "Shall I get Monique?"

She nodded yes. It was part of Monique's education. I found her with the cat.

So Céline had an audience for the first time in her life. Monique's presence worked out well, because she innocently asked a few questions, which caused her mother to relax, reflect and explain in more detail.

Olivier had said nothing the entire time, but finally he asked, "Do you think that perhaps you have received an invitation to visit the place you saw in your vision?"

"Yes...I need to go there. I always follow the directive. I have found that if I try to ignore it I inevitably become miserable. I can't speak for others though." She looked down at Monique.

"I want to go!" Monique said. "But Papa has to make sure there are no dragons in there."

I shook my head. "It looks like I have been enlisted then. One dragon slayer at your service."

Olivier chuckled. "I believe I know of the place you saw in the vision, but may we have breakfast first?"

A wise request.

That set the breakfast-Meister into motion.

It was strawberry season. I made thin crepes filled with fresh strawberries and softened cream cheese, sprinkled with powdered sugar and just a hint of dark grated chocolate. Olivier threatened to capture and keep me in his kitchen forever; a perpetual prisoner in the culinary dungeon of delights.

As we were finishing up with our coffee, he explained to Céline. "I believe the place you saw in your vision is near the Valdieu—the Valley of God. Much of the history of the Priory as well as the Knights of the Temple have played out in southwest France, near Carcassonne. The area, now only sparsely populated, was once the center of several different kingdoms, and has been important since Neolithic times. The Earth-energy there is very strong. Cold and hot springs bubble out of the ground, and both the rose-line and the Paris meridian run directly through it. The ancients considered the place a sacred site due to the powerful energy there. Now, the former seat of kingdoms is an unassuming little rural village called Rennes le Château."

"The surrounding area harbors some of the Priory's greatest secrets and serves as a site for initiation into the mysteries, as it has since well before the Templars expanded it. They carved the landscape to create an above-ground temple, which mirrors another that is below the surface. That, I think is what Céline saw."

"The place and journey of initiation has been called, 'Le Serpent Rouge', and may be experienced in a seemingly unlimited number of ways. Those with clairvoyant sensitivity may see a trail to follow. Some have said their path appears greener than the surrounding countryside. Others' initiation involves the underground temple."

"For another it can be a journey of pure spirit. There have been some that claim there is a place where time changes, or a time 'portal'. For you...who knows? It is very personal—very sacred. In my lifetime I know of only a few that have gone through an initiation there."

There was no reason for Céline, Monique and I to tarry. I gave Monsieur Lecuyer a case of the Chateau Tempier, and left the rest in his garage. Even though I felt that we had imposed on him enough already, he insisted that we return after we completed our excursion to the southwest.

Before we left, he gave me a few last minute instructions and began rummaging around in his desk drawer.

"Ah—here it is. This has been in my desk for many years now. I never needed it." He reminisced. "At one point in time these were actually used as admission into the labyrinth, and then afterwards it became kind of an informal tradition in the Priory. If you don't need it, you may pass it down to another." He handed me a very old, worn silver coin. It had a cross pateé on it.

"Is this a Templar coin?"

"French actually, but that does illustrate how much the Templars influenced the monetary system in those days."

We found our way out of Lyon and headed south along the Rhône river. At Tournon I crossed the river into Tain-l'Hermitage, where we got out and hiked up through the vineyard to the see the little chapel Olivier had described in his story the night before. It was a stiff climb, and by the time we got to the top we were winded. Céline wasn't really interested, but Monique and I wanted to see it. I had observed that it was always good for Céline to get some hard physical exercise. She had been couped up in

Monsieur Lecuyer's house for several days. Still, she was pensive, and hadn't talked much during the first leg of the drive.

As we continued the drive south along the river her mood darkened. We began to argue.

She was upset about the fact that I had not told her about the strongbox of gold, and she had been harboring resentments for several days. I admitted that I should have probably told her what my source of wealth was, but from my perspective, the day that I showed up at the Favreau home ready to formally court her I was already a man of means. She had certainly benefited from it.

From her perspective, I had not been honest with her. At first it was irritating, but then I became upset. I had done everything I could to be a good husband, including providing well for her.

It came out during the argument that she had her own bank account that she had never bothered to tell me about, inherited from her parents. In her mind, it was alright for her not to mention that to me.

It turns out that the majority of arguments married couples get in concern money. The odd thing was—we had plenty of it! It all made no sense to me, until finally it came out: I had returned to France because of the gold—not for her.

That was absurd. She was the woman of my dreams.

It was our first real heated argument, and Monique heard it all. Here we were on some kind of undefined spiritual grail quest and we ended up arguing in the car.

Since we had gotten a late start, and had made the side excursion to Hermitage, we stayed in Nimes that night. The next day we drove to Carcassonne, and got a hotel there. The town is positively steeped in history, with its old fortified walls still intact. We spent the evening as tourists in the town.

The next morning we drove through the rough, dry, rocky countryside to our destination. We picked up some picnic food in Blanchefort, and finally went into Rennes le Château.

When we got there we didn't know what to do with ourselves. Olivier's description had somehow conjured up a greater image of the place in our imagination. It appeared to be nothing more than a sleepy, rural, run-down little village out in the middle of nowhere.

Driving out of town, we found a place to rest and picnic by the river Sals. Céline spread out a blanket; promptly laid down on her back, placed a dark blue handkerchief over her eyes and fell asleep.

Monique began bouncing around investigating the environment. She splashed her hands in the water, which caused a few ducks to take off where they had been hiding nearby. The violence of their ascent frightened her at first, but then she turned, looked back and cackled. I fumbled around in the box of groceries we had purchased in Blanchefort and pulled out a baguette.

"Papa, didn't Monsieur Lecuyer say that Le Serpent Rouge could appear as a green trail? Here it is!"

I stood up and looked. "I have a good eye for trails Monique, but I don't see one there."

"It's right here. Watch—I will run down it."

The girl ran a few feet, jumped over a branch and disappeared.

19

The Jade Elephant

Monique didn't understand why her father couldn't see the trail. It was greener than the surrounding area. In fact, a few feet away, both sides of the trail flourished with greenery. She ran down it to investigate, and stumbled—skinning her knee. A year ago she would have cried, but she was a big girl now. She got up and saw her mother some distance away surrounded by a group of women. She thought that her mother was behind her, but looking that way, she saw no-one. She ran up to her mother, and grabbed her leg.

"Mama, I skinned my knee!"

One of the ladies grabbed Monique, and tried to pull her away. Her mother raised a hand and looked down at her. She asked Monique a question but it was in another language that sounded oddly familiar.

"Mama—I hurt my knee." The ladies clucked and laughed. Yvette saw recognition in her mother's face. Her mother was wearing an odd white dress. Two ladies stood nearby holding scissors, needles and thread. There were bits of white fabric on the carpet below her. Her mother picked up a small scrap and gestured to one of the ladies, who held out a goblet of wine. She dipped the material into the wine and began to clean Monique's knee.

"This might hurt a little." She spoke in an odd accent—formal, like from an old play, but Monique understood.

Her mother then studied her shoes, and her white stockings decorated with little pink elephants (Monique liked elephants). She moved the thin cotton fabric of Monique's dress between her fingers, and examined the costume-jewelry ring the girl was wearing. She then gazed over Monique's shoulder into the forest before looking back into her face. Her eyes were soft.

She spoke quietly. "Wait, I will help you. Can you wait?"

My mother doesn't recognize me. She looks so young.

Standing there, Monique began to cry—bravely.

It took the entire entourage of ladies to remove the odd white dress. They then redressed her in a blue linen dress with a thin ermine collar. Monique watched it all, fascinated—and calmed down. The entire process had occurred without her mother having to lift a finger. She just stood there while they did it all for her.

Finally they all left except for the mean, beautiful lady that had tried to pull Monique away. She also left after receiving instructions in that odd language.

Finally they were alone.

"Would you like to see my garden?"

"Yes, thank you?" Monique responded in the formal tense.

They followed a manicured pathway lined with flowers and sat down on a bench by a fountain. Bright orange fish darted around in the pool below it. They amused themselves for a brief time by tossing in some food and watching the little fish seize bits of it.

Eventually the lady spoke. "There is a powerful place in the forest where magical things happen. It is not a single place—it moves around, but it all occurs within that area over yonder." She gestured towards the trees.

"Occasionally, someone disappears there, and then returns later with tales of having visited lands with strange animals or cities with very tall buildings. Perhaps you child, have come from some other place or time."

She knelt down in front of Monique. "My name is Aliénor, and I have not yet had any children. You called me "Mama"?"

"You look like my mother."

"What is your name?"

"Monique." She was having difficulty digesting the situation, but her inquisitive nature was incorrigible.

"Why were you wearing the white dress?"

"That is to be my wedding dress."

" Who will you marry?"

"Prince Louis Capet." She looked off to the side.

"Are you a princess?"

"Yes."

"Don't you want to marry him?"

Aliénor looked down and then back up at Monique. "Sometimes there are things we simply must do."

Monique did not understand, but sensed that she should not query further.

"Monique, are there princes where you come from?"

"Yes, there's Prince Charles of England. He's a baby."

"Is there a King of England?"

"I don't know. There's a Queen of England."

They sat there for awhile in silence watching the fish,

until an old women in a rough white linen robe joined them. Aliénor stood up as a sign of respect, and Monique instinctively followed suit. Aliénor made the introductions in both languages. The elderly women's name was Dora, and Monique was told that she knew all about the magical ways of the forest. They talked in their language for awhile, until Dora got up, took Monique's hands in her own gnarled ones, squeezed them, smiled, and walked away.

"The wise woman has told me that we should be able to return you to your parents, but we will have to wait until this evening. Would you like to have dinner with us?"

"Yes, thank you."

They left the garden and made their way through a maze of entrances and hallways. There were soldiers standing guard with tall spears and swords at their sides. Aliénor's suite was luxurious, with thick floral designed carpets on the floors. While the lady busied herself with needlework, Monique played with a young cat. Suddenly her stomach began to feel sick.

"Aliénor? There is a bad man that is coming here that means to do you harm."

The needle stopped. She stared down at Monique, who was kneeling on the floor. Presently, there was a knock on the door. Monique fled and hid behind a screen. The mean, beautiful lady came in and announced a visitor. She seemed proud and excited. When the lady left to show him in, Monique watched as Aliénor slipped a thin dagger up her left sleeve—the hilt hidden by a lace cuff.

The visitor entered first, followed by the lady. He was all fluff and finery, and a very handsome man. He emanated a demeanor of confidence and congeniality—one of Aliénor's inner circle. He was a man that could be trusted.

Monique was very frightened by him. She found him repulsive like one would be towards a rabid animal or a venomous snake. She was beginning to trust her intuition. It was a similar feeling to the one she had when there were bad men at the château.

They drank some wine and chatted in Old French. Monique didn't understand some of it, but the tone was friendly and casual.

After they left, Aliénor sat down at a desk, and with a quill and inkwell wrote on a piece of parchment. Monique emerged from her hiding place to watch as the lady dripped some red wax on it and carefully pressed a stamp into the wax. She then turned and looked at Monique.

"Why were you afraid of Robert de Guillaume?"

Yvette didn't know how to express it.

"Robert is one of my confidants, and has done some good work for me."

Monique responded, "It was kind of like when we were going to our home, and I knew there were some bad men waiting there."

"Were they truly bad, or was it just your imagination?"

"Well... They killed my Uncle Xavier."

Aliénor's accusation hurt her feelings, and thinking of Uncle Xavier caused Monique to start to cry.

Aliénor softened. "I'm sorry to hear about your uncle."

She poured a little wine into a cup, filled it the rest of the way with water and handed it to Monique.

"Drink this." It tasted bad. Monique made a face when she drank it. She didn't like wine, but she realized that she had been thirsty. "Are you tired? You may sleep for awhile on my bed if you wish."

Aliénor's bed was soft and smelled of lavender.

When Monique awoke, her host was sitting on the other side of the suite in front of a tall, narrow arched window. A flagon and a goblet rested on the small table in front of her with a shaft of sunlight shining on it. The ladies's face was in the shadows, but the light sparkled off of the golden goblet as she slowly, thoughtfully rotated it by its stem.

Monique was groggy after the nap. *She's so beautiful. She's a real princess, and she needs help!* Monique rubbed her eyes and went over to her.

"Monique, you may have done me a great service. I have a small gift for you—something to remember me by."

She produced a little sewn leather case with a white shell button, and handed it to Yvette, who struggled with the button. The case contained a miniature elephant, carved in green jade.

"It is from a far away land, where animals like this live."

Monique thanked her.

Not long after that a servant brought a meal for them both. Each serving was a small loaf of brownish bread that had been cut in half, hollowed out, and filled with a kind of stew. It was served on a board. There were no plates, forks, or spoons. There were only knives. Monique didn't know quite what to do with it, so she ate some of the cheese that came on a separate board, and watched how her host skillfully dealt with it with a knife and her hands. It was messy. Monique didn't really care, and was hungry, so she ate much of it the same way Aliénor did. It was great fun. When they were done they wiped themselves off with a wet cloth, and a servant took the mess away.

All that was left on the table was the little elephant,

who she had placed there at the beginning of the meal. She figured he would be amused by their antics.

When the sun was beginning to set, old Dora showed up, and they retraced their steps through the hallways, past the soldiers and out into the gardens. At the edge of the forest Dora stopped and waited. When the sun had fully set the old woman began to move forward and to the left. The light from the sun still illuminated the undersides of puffy clouds far in the distance. Denizens of frogs were singing a powerful symphony that blotted out other sounds. Dora seemed unsure as to which way to go. Monique could see the green trail clearly. She pulled on the old ladies dress and pointed.

"It's right there."

Dora looked down at her and said in her own language, "You can see it can't you?"

Monique understood, and nodded her head.

Aliénor suddenly felt a pang of regret and panic.

We are sending a five-year old girl into the forest alone at night?

Dora caught the thought. "She will be fine m'lady. Her mother is on the other side of the gate. I can see her aura. It looks like the child's."

Aliénor bent down and gave Monique a hug. "Go now child, while you still can."

Monique turned and ran down the trail, pausing to turn and wave before she went through the portal. She could see it clearly. It was teeming with the little people of the forest. She plunged through and fell, this time skinning her hands.

Her mother was still sleeping in the shade beneath the oak tree.

My child is with me now.
She is dabbling her feet in the river.
He is lost in the darkness,
The realm I was once enamored with.
It beckons to me still.
But he is a light being,
Unfamiliar with the labyrinth of despair.
He is of the sky—of the sun.
For him, shadows dwell in the corner of an afternoon.
The darkness is merely an interruption of the sunlight.
I sense that he must however,
Find and conquer the darkness, his nemesis.
When he emerges from the Labyrinth,
He will wield a greater sword,
And enter the world of light as a more powerful being.
I shall wait and sleep,
Sheltered under grandfather oak,
And protected by the people of the forest.

20

The Iron Door

When Monique disappeared I thought she had fallen into a hole. I ran to where she had jumped over the arm-sized branch. There was no hole. I kicked the branch. Alarmed, I moved in the direction she had been going.

I was knocked to my knees by what felt like a mattress coming down on my head and shoulders. I found myself looking down at flat dusty ground, and at the same time my nose picked up the unmistakable odor of human filth. Looking up, I saw a rectangle of azure-blue twilight sky, with a few stars beginning to peek out. As my eyes began to adjust to the dark, I could see that what formed the rectangle were actually very tall stone walls. I was kneeling in the middle of a courtyard.

From behind me came a rough, low cry of alarm, a shuffling and an odd, dry squeaking sound. As I turned to look I slipped my hand in my jacket pocket on my pistol, and realized what had made that sound. It was a well used bow being drawn. A rough looking character in an archer's stance had an arrow trained on me.

He was soon joined by others. They all looked similar: medieval soldiers in leather armor.

It is an odd thing how the human mind works. If we are confronted with a situation with too much unexplained phenomenon attached to it the mind will endeavor to fit it into a known thought pattern.

When Monique disappeared, I saw it as her falling into a hole. She *disappeared*. Even though it's embarrassing for me to admit; when I was surrounded by those medieval soldiers—for a moment I thought I must be on a movie set. It was the only thing that made sense to my mind. My senses however, prevailed. They had weapons trained on me, and no modern actors smelled like those men did.

One of them produced a torch, and held it out over me. Some of the oil from it dripped on the dust in front of me. Their eyes glistened with fear in the torchlight.

They are afraid to kill me. They think I am a demon.

The soldiers looked emaciated, as if they hadn't eaten in days. We were starting to attract a crowd.

A higher pitched man's voice called out a command from the building. Some of the soldiers lowered their weapons and stood aside while a small old man in a dirty white robe pushed through. He considered me for a moment, then asked a question in a language not familiar to me.

I replied slowly in French. "I am Marc Rémillard. I am looking for my daughter—a little girl."

He understood. "There are no young children here." His French was archaic. He held his hand up, and the soldiers lowered their weapons. I put my right palm on the ground and slowly stood up. I still held the baguette in my left hand.

He studied me carefully. I was dressed for a vacation: a jacket, slacks, and a button-down shirt with a collar. I had short hair. Their hair was all long and greasy.

"Are you a warrior?"

I hesitated. "I was a soldier once."

He moved closer and looked up directly into my eyes. "I had a waking dream that we would be visited by a warrior from afar. One who carries a powerful weapon."

I thought of the pistol still concealed in my jacket. I wouldn't really consider it described as a powerful weapon. They might though. But I was not going to show it to them. With his hand and a word he gestured for me to accompany him into a building.

We climbed up a series of spiral stone steps until we came to his room in the tower. From there the last hint of the sunset was still visible. The trappings in his room were not those of a soldier. There were stacks of scrolls, an abacus, a lute, and an odd little flat viol.

"Pardon my rudeness in this late hour. I am Betrand Marty. Your name—Rémillard? You are of the family of a high king?"

"No, its just my name."

He regarded me for a moment. He looked like he hadn't slept for days.

"We can drink the last of my wine. Is that bread you are carrying?"

"Yes, I would be glad to share it with you."

He fumbled with a small cask with a wooden bung protruding from it. He tipped it to get the last of the wine out.

"Will you help me?"

We managed to fill two cups with the red wine. It had quite a bit of sediment in it. I broke the baguette in half and placed it on the table amongst the writing implements. He tore off a small piece of it.

"I have never seen bread like this—so white."

He then performed a ritual that I have since seen a depiction of Methuselah doing in front of Chartres cathedral. He closed his eyes, dipped the bread into the wine and recited a prayer in his own language. He then slowly ate the bread and took a drink of the wine before opening his eyes.

The wine was turning to vinegar, but I drank it anyway. At home I would pour wine like that out. I was not at home.

"Good bread. My last I fear. I thought, because of the dream that we might at last be saved from the armies of King Louis."

"Armies?"

"Yes, the French armies camped outside of the walls. We have agreed to surrender tomorrow."

"Where, may I ask are we?"

He looked at me long and hard; his eyes flickering back and forth. "The citadel of Montségur."

I vaguely remembered that the siege of Montségur was the last in a campaign to eliminate the heretical Cathars.

"You are a Cathar?"

"I am the head of the Perfecti."

He became lost in his thoughts for awhile. Finally he spoke, "Do you bear a weapon as I saw in the dream?"

"I have a weapon, but it is not powerful enough to defeat an army, only a few assailants."

"Could it serve to protect one person?"

"Yes, but it can be used only eight times. Also, I may have once served as a soldier, but I must have a reason to fight. I have no wish to kill men unnecessarily."

From that statement I perceived that I had gained his respect.

"How did you come to be here?"

I had nothing to loose by being completely honest with him.

"I herald from what would be your future. I, my wife and our child were on a kind of quest—in a place we call Rennes le Château, near Blanchefort. We were seeking Le Serpent Rouge—a place of initiation. My daughter ran down a trail and disappeared. When I searched for her, I found myself here."

He took a few moments to process that.

"I know of such a place. It is not far from here. It is an ancient sacred site used for the purposes of initiation into the mysteries, and now controlled by the Knights of the Temple.

"Are the Knights of the Temple the enemies of the Cathars?"

"They have fashioned an uncomfortably neutral position. If they had not, it would have ended in their demise."

"Why have the French armies attacked the Cathars?"

"Attacked? In the last 36 years they have managed to commit genocide upon an entire culture. It was the most enlightened society in Europe. Because of our tolerance of all peoples, our merchants were the wealthiest, our poets the most profound, and our art and music was the sensation of Europe. The popular music of the troubadours created an entire new way of thinking and teaching. The music from our monasteries sang of joy, which was poorly emulated in the north with their dull chants. The northern French were envious of all of those attributes—and wanted the wealth for themselves."

He paused and then continued. "The teachings of the Perfecti were threatening to the doctrine of the Church of Rome. We taught that every man, and every woman from all nations are all—at their essence—paratge. Our struggle as men is to realize it and work towards purity and perfection. It was the Church of Rome that was behind the genocide of my brothers and sisters."

"In the fields and in the forests I taught tolerance and love for all people. I spoke against war and hatred. We believed in a society without war, without an army to protect us—all while living in the midst of a hostile world. It was a foolish, idealistic stance."

"Teacher. You may not want to hear this, but the war that I fought in occurs seven hundred years into your future, and was called World War II. Only a few years before that, there was another huge war: World War I which ironically was termed 'The war to end all wars'."

"An entire world at war? It grieves me to hear that."

194

He stared down at the table for some time.

He then spoke more calmly. "One of my favorite themes when I taught was tolerance, and its child—forgiveness. I could see no place for hatred. I had observed how it could consume the life energy of a person. Now I am the worst kind of hypocrite, because I hate the Church of Rome. It has become my archenemy. I cannot forgive its crimes. The more I try to purge the hatred from my soul the further entrenched it becomes."

"On this night—the eve of the death of my physical body, perhaps it is appropriate for you—man of the future, to be my confessor, my confidant."

He drank the last of his wine.

"We are surrounded and besieged by evil. I see no paratge on the bleak horizons."

"Paratge?"

"You know not of paratge? Is there no honor and decency in your society in the future? Do you live like animals feeding off of each other?"

"There is still much honor and decency in my time."

He studied me for a moment, and then shifted into a well-practiced teachers mode. He explained it to me in a simplified form—like he was needing to teach a child how to eat. I perceived that the concept was lodged at the core of his being, and central to his near-extinct society.

"In its most elemental form, paratge is expressed by those who endeavor to always do what they believe is the right thing to do, following the tenants of honor, truth, decency, and kindness. That in itself, is a model for a healthy society, but paratge can be expressed and manifests itself on different evolving levels. As the levels increase in consciousness the fabric of life becomes both finer and stronger."

"A mother protects her children, a man actively shields his family, and in turn a Count is honor-bound to protect those in his county from harm—like my lord the Count of Toulouse, where I served as bishop. Our scholars debated whether or not war itself ran contrary to the righteous path. Now I think that those that argued against a standing army were childless, and did not understand what any good parent knows."

"You are a parent, and have braved the labyrinth of the past in search of your daughter. I say you are living in paratge of a higher order."

He continued, "A king's righteous role is as a shepherd and protector of his subjects, who ultimately prosper in peace. The Grail King is himself a high initiate on the path of the spirit. With his sword-hand squarely on the tiller, he peers through the mist into the future, guiding his ship safely through waters both calm and peaceful— and stormy and treacherous."

"This hearkens from our ancestors, the mystic Kings of the Mérovée, from their ancestors in Arcadia, and much further into the past."

"At its highest manifestation, paratge is an individuals' journey towards seeking the divinity within him or herself. It is the initiates' return to God. We are all essentially gods who have forgotten whence we came."

"But now it comes down to this. I have very little hope left."

"Totz lo mons Ne valg mens, de ver o sapiatz, car Paratges

Ne Fo destruitz e decassatz. E totz Crestianesmes aonitz
e abassatz".

He translated from Occitan:

"It diminished the whole world, be sure of that, for
it destroyed and drove out paratge. It disgraced and
shamed all Christendom.

[From the Song of the Cathar Wars, Laisse 137 and Laisse 141]

"Perhaps we can help each other. You are close to the
bloodline are you not?"

"Yes."

"Would you consider helping a royal member—one
of your ancestors shall we say, escape from this fortress
tonight? We will see that you return to the serpent
labyrinth."

My alternatives were grim. I agreed.

"I will ask but one favor of you. I will write a testament
of these times for you to take with you into the future;
assuming you are skilled enough to find your way back.
I will also write a brief letter of introduction to the
Templar commander for you. It is he who guards the
labyrinth. The Order has, at great expense sculpted the
landscape in a vast area to create it for reasons they keep
secret."

He moved to a small writing desk that was set at an
angle—like a podium. With quill and ink he carefully
drafted a document, and a letter. When he was finished,
he dried them over a candle, handed me the letter, rolled
up the document, and slipped it into a wooden tube
with a shoulder strap. I watched as he nervously fussed
around with a few things.

"We have tarried here long enough. They are waiting."

After descending the spiral staircase, we moved down a short hallway, where he knocked on a heavy wooden door. It was opened by a small wiry young man with a pointed nose and quick, dreamy eyes. There was a coil of rope on the floor. A dignified older woman dressed in garb similar to those of my host stood nearby.

He formally introduced her to me. "Marc Rémillard, this is Rixende de Telle."

She looked right through me. It was unnerving. They waited until she gave me a minute smile and nodded her head in approval.

The fourth person in the room was a younger woman. When she moved out of the shadows I gasped, and moved forward towards her. "Céline?"

She put her hand up in a defensive gesture. The small man moved close to her as if to protect her. He put his hand on the pommel of the rapier hanging at his side. She was taller than he was. Strong words began to rapidly fly between the young lady and the old teacher. When the young man tried to speak, she silenced him. I got a good, clear truth picture.

The little man is infatuated with her. He adored, and idolized her, and fantasized having her as his own. He was playing out a favorite theme of the Troubadours— unrequited love, bound by irony. Gwenevere and Lancelot loved each other. They could not be together, but she kept him close. They both loved Arthur, who in turn loved both of them—and he knew! A classic Troubadour tale.

This lady would not allow the man to be her lover,

but kept him close so she could feed off of his adoration. She needed love, but refused to admit it—even to herself. He was the only person she truly trusted, because she knew what drove him.

She was not Céline, but bore a remarkable resemblance to her.

There was a pause in the argument, and I broke in—calmly, "Lady, I apologize, but you look like my wife."

"I am not your *wife*." She switched to the same archaic French the old teacher used.

"I know that now! Please allow me to show you something."

I pulled my wallet out of my back pocket. The rapier rose partway out of it's scabbard. I removed a small black & white photograph of Monique, and handed it to her. I felt a surge of panic when I remembered that my little Monique was lost.

"I am searching for my daughter. This is a picture of her."

They crowded together and—speechless, stared at the photograph of Monique at the beach with a little bucket in one hand and a plastic trowel in the other. They didn't know what to make of it. Then I handed them a close-up picture of Céline that I was particularly proud of. I had been playing around with a Roloflex camera that I had purchased in Geneva. The men were standing on either side of her. Both of them looked up at her and the young man spoke. I didn't understand his language but I knew what he said. This woman and Céline could be identical twins.

199

I had successfully diffused the situation for the moment.

The young man addressed me, "Are you a warrior?"

I didn't like his tone, so I threw it back at him. "Yes. Are you a warrior?"

"I am a poet," he said proudly, as if poets had a higher status than a mere soldier.

I turned and looked at the old teacher. *I am to protect a prima dona and a poet?*

He got it. "Tomas knows the escape route, and the way to the Templar keep."

I did not want to engage in a verbal cock-fight with the poet.

"Excellent." I nodded to the poet.

The lady wasn't satisfied. "How do we know that you can protect me?"

"Me?" Not "We"? The lady was accustomed to being the center of attention. Was her poet-companion a mere disposable commodity?

"I am fully capable to protect you and Tomas." *I added him to her list.*

"You bear no weapon."

"I do."

"May I see it?"

I hesitated. Perhaps a show and tell would not be a bad idea. If I had to use it they needed to be prepared for it. I pulled the pistol out of my jacket, removed the magazine, and extracted one of the .32 caliber cartridges. I had never fired the Walther PP. The cartridges were the same ones that were in it when I got it: deluxe, German-made, with shiny nickel-plated casings, and copper-tipped bullets. It held nine rounds, but one was missing due to the SS officer taking a pot-shot at me.

"This is like an arrow, but flies much faster. It will kill one man. There are eight of these in the weapon. If I use the weapon, it will make a very loud sound. Please do not be alarmed."

Their silent reaction was predictable. Somehow I felt protective of these people. They were like children living and loving life—but existing in a harsh time. I feel that we, in the 21st century, have evolved socially. We no longer accept the idea that armies can run wild over the landscape—rape, pillage and burn as they systematically did in the middle ages.

I realized that if the three of us were to survive a very dangerous mission, we would need to be coalesced as a team. I wanted them to be firmly on my side.

The poet had given me an idea. It was absurd, but the situation reminded me of the movies and plays called "musicals" in the modern world—when one never knows when an actor will spontaneously break-into-song.

I announced dramatically, "Before we leave, I will recite a poem."

My comrades-in-arms in the 20th century would have laughed and told me to shut-up, but not this group from the 13th century. These people were steeped in and driven by art. They were of a culture that, on the eve of their destruction, when hostile forces outside the walls were ready to chop them up and burn the pieces—would pause and listen to poetry.

Besides, I liked my poem, and for once had a willing audience. They waited politely.

In ancient days they tell a tale
Of restless wanderers under lofty sail
Who left their land they loved so dear
To crashing waves and nameless fear

With them they brought their wisdom old
Their fortunes not for time untold
To build anew—a shining star
In ruddy land of oak and brier

The stones they set in circle wide
A fairy ring—of giants stride
For them—time and place
Was brightest sun and deepest space

So on and on generations passed
Doubt not 'oh children, for wisdom lasts
A golden thread that weaves through time
Of elven fabric—like this cloak of mine

So as I ponder—wine in hand
Of future days and far off lands
I leave this place—only to return
As my fire dies, and midnight yearns

The old man was truly touched. I addressed him. "Perfect. Your teachings have not been in vain."
"Will you take paratge with you?"
"It would be my honor, teacher."

"Farewell—man of the future."

Both Tomas and the lady then received specific instructions and goodbye's from him and Rixende de Telle. Under a heavy table in the corner was a discreet hatch in the floor with a stone lid. Tomas led, the lady followed, and I took up the rear and carried the rope. I looked up as the teacher muscled the lid back into place.

The tunnel went down at a steep angle. We passed through a horizontal iron hatch, and crawled through a section that had been hammered out of the rock at unnatural angles. Finally, Tomas extinguished his candle as we approached the opening, which had been purposefully blocked by a stone. He struggled with it until I moved forward and managed to roll it back out of the way. An oval of stars appeared as the night air gushed through the opening. I could smell the smoke from the fires of the besiegers. A heavy iron ring had been embedded into the wall. With the rope I lowered the poet down first, and then the lady, who carried a carefully wrapped bundle. I then went down hand over hand about fifty feet to where they were waiting. I insisted upon cutting off the last small section of rope and coiled it around my waist.

We moved down the steep slope with little cover except for a few bushes and large rocks. There was just enough moonlight to see a person moving over the landscape. The lady and I hid close in the shadow of a rock while Tomas searched for what I gathered was another opening.

I got a truth picture, but it was not preceded by a visual image. Perhaps it was just a sense.

The lady was attracted to me. In the darkness, she was

struggling not to reach out and touch me.

I was not surprised, as I was now perceived as a man of power. Beautiful women are attracted to men of power like moths to flames. The women live in a kind of void of loneliness. They often have few lady friends. Other women instinctively resent and hate them, while men either idolize or are aggressive towards them. Beautiful women thus build up a series of personal shields to protect themselves, which in turn serve to increase their isolation. Men of power are seen as protectors, and providers of luxury and a quality life style.

I would ignore it, but my eyes were open. *I could feel the hand from her astral body on my shoulder.*

As we waited for Tomas, I wondered if my truth picture sensitivity was evolving.

I observed Tomas as he approached us. He was stealthy, and moved like a cat. I was beginning to have more respect for him.

"Come, I found it." He said

Behind a thorn bush was the opening to a cave. We groped in until Tomas stopped and began fumbling with what I eventually realized was a tinder box. I don't think he was particularly skilled at operating the device.

"Wait, I will light the candle."

Prudent old boy scout that I was, I usually carried a book of matches in my coat pocket. I pulled out one that I had picked up at our casino hotel at the Riviera. It was large, flamboyant, red, and depicted three scantily clad women performing the can-can. The break-off matches were made of wood. I lit the candle as he held it out.

We were in a natural cave system, which continued erratically underground. In places the rock had been carved out to facilitate passage through. For the most part Tomas remembered the way, but several times we had to retrace our steps and try another route. After several hours of scrambling over rocks and squeezing through tight passageways we came to the end of the tunnel. It emerged on the side of a hill. It was a gray dawn, but the top of the fortress walls of Montségur could be seen between the hills in the distance. We were still in dangerous territory. I was exhausted and hungry, and my companions appeared even more so. By modern standards they would be considered malnourished. At least I had insisted that we pause and drink from one of the underground streams in the caves that seemed to have pure water in it.

"Perhaps we should rest here in the mouth of the cave until nightfall." I suggested.

"We must keep moving. Today the armies will begin to disseminate, after the surrender." Tomas insisted.

We headed due west through the dry, brushy, rocky countryside. Presently we came to a deserted farm. The house had been burnt down, but I spied a scrawny brown and black chicken scurry across the clearing. She had miraculously survived the hungry marauding soldiers. She hid well, but we managed to find a considerable clutch of eggs—nine in all. All that was left of the house was the blackened fireplace with a cauldron hanging in it.

It was risky, but we had to eat. I started a quick fire with as much small tinder as we could gather, drew some water out of the well, and boiled the eggs in the cauldron. We took the hot eggs with us and ate them once we were well away from that place.

By noon, the effects of exhaustion on my companions

was obvious. Neither of them were accustomed to heavy physical exertion. The lady would not let either of us carry the package that she had slung over her shoulder on a leather strap. She was stumbling over stones, and the poet was driving himself too hard. I insisted that we stop to rest. I chose a small clearing surrounded by bushes and trees, but I failed to perform due diligence. A soldier should always scout the area before bedding down.

We were only a stone's throw from a road with wheel ruts in it.

I awoke to a scuffing sound. The lady was struggling with a man, while another brigand was entering the other side of the clearing. I pulled out my pistol, but couldn't get a clear shot at the ruffian strangling her because she was wrestling with him, even after he had her by the neck with a long, ugly knife to her throat. She continued to struggle, until suddenly his mouth opened and his eyes bulged out. The tip of a rapier appeared, protruding out from under his chin. I bolted forward, grabbed the knife, and pushed him backwards so he wouldn't fall on the lady. I then twirled and trained my pistol on the other man. He was very young—perhaps only fifteen. My fighting stance and lack of fear of him scared him, and he fled.

The poet had appeared out of nowhere. He had woken up, and gone off to relieve himself when the men attacked. Now he stood over the fallen man with his bloodied sword. He was breathing hard, and didn't seem to know what to do with the rapier. Finally, he cleaned it on the fallen brigand's filthy tunic and returned it to its scabbard. Tomas had done it—he had killed a man. He had saved her. He was the hero that he had dreamed he could be. I pretended not to notice when, several minutes later he went behind a rock and vomited.

The lady became catatonic, and knelt down. I left them both to calm down for a minute while I scouted the area for more trouble. It was then that I found the road. When I returned she was still staring at the ground. I knelt in front of her, and put a hand on her arm. "Lady, we are not harmed. Tomas has saved you."

She looked up at him. The poet's face was a defenseless watercolor of emotions.

"Thank you Tomas," she said in Occitan.

After a few moments, I steered them out of their reverie by addressing him. "Tomas—there is a road over there."

"I will look."

He recognized the road, and knew where we were. "We will not follow the road, but continue through the woodlands on the other side of it. We may be able to reach Chateau Templier by nightfall."

We moved like hunters, quietly through the forest, and with stealth through the open areas. At dusk we still had some distance to go, so decided to stop and wait until morning. This time we found a safe place to bed down.

They conversed for a while in Occitan. I was beginning to understand a bit of it. It was related to French but had a clipped cadence, similar to the Basque I had heard from some of the workers we had hired to help pick our grapes. I gathered that they were headed for a place called Usson.

I awoke at bird-time, when it's not quite light enough for them to move about, but they unanimously make their presence known by calling out with fervor. Why they do that I do not know, but it only happens for about five minutes.

The lady slept in. Tomas would not wake her, which was probably best. Let her sleep. I was parched with thirst, so I scouted around until I found a spring in a greener area on top of a hill nearby. From there I had a view of the surrounding countryside. I sat up there for awhile, filling my stomach with the spring water. There was no need to hurry. I figured the lady was a sleeper, like Céline.

My wife was a night-owl, staying up late and sleeping until late morning. She had the luxury to do so. I couldn't understand it, because for me my mornings are the best of times. Monique had temporarily altered Céline's habits, but when I appeared on the scene she went back to sleeping in.

My mornings with my daughter were precious. I had decided early on that breakfasts for us were to be a sacred time. If I was displeased with something Monique did or needed to do, I would not bring the subject up during breakfast. It was a time-out for all parental nagging.

From the hill-top perch I could see a fort in the distance. When I returned to camp I described it to Tomas, who said it was probably Chateau Templier. He was not willing to get too close to it, but when we moved out we went in that direction until he was certain that it was, in fact my destination.

They had honored their commitment to me. Paratge still lived.

In the short time I had spent with the two of them I'd become quite fond of them both. I looked at the lady straight on, spoke to her, and at the same time sent her a mental message.

"Be careful lady." *Be careful of your heart.*

Her eyes fluttered before she threw up an emotional shield. She hadn't known I was aware that she was attracted to me.

I turned to Tomas. "Will you compose a poem about this Tomas?"

"Perhaps." *That was a yes.*

"Farewell."

"Farewell Marc."

I never found out her name. I was not supposed to be privy to that detail.

They headed off to the south. I was a soldier again, and squatted down to reconnoiter the situation, survey the area, and form a strategy.

I tried to recall everything I knew about the Templars. It wasn't much. Raoul had told me that the Templars created the basis for the banking institutions that we know today, with checks and credit. He said that they had become so wealthy that they loaned money to kings. That, in fact was one of the reasons agents of the French King Philip IV arrested them in 1307. The French court was, of course famous for its excesses. The kingdom was bankrupt, and owed the Templars more money than the King could (or wanted to) pay back.

It was also an opportunity to seize the Order's massive hoard of gold, but the King was thwarted in that attempt. The Templars managed to sneak it out of the country before Philip could get his greedy hands on it.

Raoul also told me that the way the Templar order was structured became the basis for 20th century financial trusts. "Own nothing but control everything". In contrast to the extreme wealth of the order, Templar knights took vows of personal poverty and chastity. Raoul had snickered at that, because it did not mean that they avoided luxuries. The order controlled vast estates, particularly vineyards in southern France. "To drink like a Templar" is still a common expression in France.

I had somehow found myself in 1244, when the Templar order was at the apex of it's power. I remembered that they formed skilled, disciplined fighting forces that would fight to the death if necessary—and their belief systems were religiously eccentric.

Any organization is composed of members of varied beliefs, strengths and weaknesses—and gravitate towards different levels: there are those that carry the chamber pots and those that command legions. Whoever the commander of Chateau Templier was, he was in control of perhaps the most esoteric entity in the order: *Le Serpent Rouge*. He had to be someone special.

I decided that my best strategy was to be direct, powerful, and honest, but avoid religious discussions. I took out the letter of introduction Betrand Marty had written for me. It was brief, in Latin, and somehow looked familiar. I put it in the handkerchief pocket of my jacket where I could produce it easily without the threat of pulling a weapon.

The keep towered above the surrounding area, built on a defensive hilltop position, with cultivated fields in the valley below. The peasants eyed me warily. I ignored them, and strode down the middle of the road fearlessly and with purpose. It was an act difficult to maintain, particularly when a dry wind began blowing.

I felt vulnerable and exposed. My feet slipped on the rocks as I climbed the steep approach to the fort. The percussive slap of my hard soled shoes on the wooden drawbridge was muffled by the wind. Finally I stood in front of the entrance, alone like an ant looking up at it.

The massive doors of the Templar keep were closed.

I stood, with my hands clasped in front of my pelvis, like a performer waiting while others perform. A bearded head appeared on the top of the wall. He yelled at me. Unintelligible. It was not a question—more of a jeer.

I drew the letter out of my jacket and held it up. "I bear a letter for your commander." I held the folded letter tightly as it fluttered like a pendant in the wind. He called to someone else on the other side of the wall. After a minute an iron hatch with an arrow slit in it about twenty feet above me opened and another bearded head poked out.

I repeated, "I bear a letter for your commander." I was not riding a horse as a typical messenger would be, but literacy was certainly something to be taken seriously in that era.

He studied me, and replied in French. "My orders are not to allow visitors to enter today." His head disappeared and a strong hand reached out to pull the hatch shut.

"I seek Le Serpent Rouge!" I said clearly.

The hatch remained open, the sergeant's head came out again, and he studied me more carefully. He was vacillating. *At what point must a good soldier choose to disobey orders and act on his own accord?*

"What Order do you represent?"

Order?

"I am of the Order of the Purple Hand!" I said proudly.

211

That did it. They ushered me in through the postern gate. They were all business. The sergeant informed me that the commander was away, but should return that day. I was shown to an outdoor covered area where I was told to wait. It was next to the stables, and built in the same fashion: with straw on the floor, a chest-high railing, and several benches on which to sit. The horse-railing was curious. I could have jumped over it, but it was apparently there to keep me from wandering around the compound.

They were in the habit of showing hospitality to pilgrims. This was a place where they could rest, and spend the night before continuing onward.

I was the only solitary pilgrim in the waiting area. A few minutes later a servant brought me food. It was obviously a routine he had performed hundreds of times. It was a kind of unsalted porridge mixed with animal fat, and an older—hard piece of bread to eat it with. From somewhere in my memory I recalled what it was termed: "gruel"—the most common food for people in the European middle ages. I ate it.

I spent much of the day watching the common people and the soldiers going about their business, and the blacksmith across from me dogmatically heating a piece of iron in the forge and then hammering it on the anvil. His son helped him with the bellows and stoked the forge. They worked almost wordlessly, mostly shoeing the horses in the stables next to me.

Towards the end of the day they began to work with a longer piece of iron. The mood of the father-son team changed subtly. The blacksmith was working on a pet project, and the boy was excited about it.

212

He would like to be known as a famous sword-maker.

He held the piece in the forge, while his son watched. "Now?" His son asked.

"Wait...a bit longer."

He pulled it out, folded and hammered it, before repeating the process again and again. By the end of their work day the sword was still far from completed, but it was beginning to look like one. They discussed it, in Occitan. I got the gist of it. The blacksmith was teaching his son, but he was not yet a master sword-maker. They were both learning. His son was spirited and bright. They needed to get a higher temperature out of their forge, and the boy had a few ideas about how to achieve it.

After they left for the day I realized that I had enjoyed watching the exchange between the father and his son. I would like to have a son of my own—but first I must find my daughter.

The pilgrim area was cleverly situated so that the comings and goings from the castle could not be observed from there. Spies can be easily disguised as pilgrims.

I was not aware the commander had arrived, but was eventually shown to his quarters.

"Thank you for receiving me. I trust your sergeant will not be demerited for allowing me in this morning."

"I award initiative in my command, as long as a soldier's assessments are correct!" He raised his eyebrows.

"And that remains to be determined?" I was engaging him in a bit of friendly verbal swordplay.

"Yes." His reply was edged, but not without humor.

"I am Marc Rémillard."

"Raymond de Bures."

He studied me for a moment. My suit coat was of a

style that was popular in 1949, with broad padded shoulders and a narrow straight waist, which extended down to the crotch. It was dark gray wool with fine subtle blue pinstripes.

He was younger than I had expected—less than forty, with cropped sandy blond hair and a trimmed beard. He was tall and elegant, with unreadable light blue eyes that seemed to be focused far into space.

"I am told you seek Le Serpent Rouge?"

"Yes."

"That is an unusual request—if in fact such an entity exists."

"I have a letter of introduction from Betrand Marty." I held it out to him. He paused for a moment while my arm was stretched out, looked at the letter as if it were tainted, then finally took it.

He quickly read it, then turned his head to the side with the letter still in his hand.

"They burned them all."

"Excuse me?"

"I have just returned from Montségur."

I said nothing, but for a moment stared into those steely eyes. *This man is a lot like me. He feels it as well.*

He had momentarily let his guard down.

"Who are you? It says here you are a warrior."

"I was a soldier."

"Once a warrior always a warrior. For whom did you fight?"

"I fought for my country."

"May I ask what country?"

"One that you have not heard of, that will be located on a continent that you may not be aware exists."

"Try me."

I pointed to the west. "There are huge lands on the other side of the Atlantic ocean."

"I am aware of the land there. We have sent ships, as did the Celts before us."

This guy was tough—used to gathering as much information as he could, while providing little. That last bit took me by surprise though.

I went on the aggressive. "Commander, have you ever heard about an element of the Serpent Rouge that involves changes of time?"

"I am not at liberty to discuss such matters."

"I am. I was born in the year one thousand nine hundred and twenty three. In my time, I live north of where the Rhône river comes out of the mountains, turns and heads south towards the Mediterranean. I was instructed to search for Le Serpent Rouge attended by my wife and young daughter. We traveled to this environs, and stopped to rest by the river Sals. We rested near a large stone that has Celtic symbols on it and had been carved into the shape of a huge chair."

Behind his poker face I sensed recognition.

"We were told that the sacred path could appear greener than the surrounding environment. My five year old daughter claimed she could see it, began running down it, and promptly disappeared. When I ran to find her, I was knocked to the ground, and found myself at the citadel of Montségur in the year one thousand two-hundred and forty-four."

"You asked me if I were a warrior. I am now again because I am searching for my daughter. You may not be able to relate to that unless you have sired children."

215

He looked down. "I wouldn't be so hasty to judge. I too had a daughter once."

Hard—stoic—pain. She died in a plague.

He held my gaze in a kind of a challenge, but one filled with complex emotions. I could tell he avoided having to take a defensive position. "Who sent you to find Le Serpent Rouge?"

"A high ranking member of an organization called, in my time the Prieuré de Sion."

His body language changed.

"He gave me this as a token for passage into the labyrinth." Reaching into my trouser's pocket, I pulled out several coins, and handed him the silver piece with the Templar cross patté on one side and a castle on the reverse side. As he was studying it I added, "You know, I think that I am already in the labyrinth; my journey began at Montségur.

"I do not recognize this coin." *Squinting—his close-up eyesight was poor.* "It is French. Philip the fourth? There is no such King. A forgery."

"There will be. It hasn't been minted yet. Philip le Bel was the French King when the Templars were..." *I mustn't tell him*, "It's in your future. Look at these." I handed him two common modern French coins, one a one franc piece.

"Can you read the date? It says one thousand nine hundred and forty eight." Compared to the crudely minted medieval silver gros tournois, the detail on the modern French coin was superb, with a rendition of a lovely, powerful goddess in neoclassical attire. I could see he was thinking about it, but still not convinced. I unbuckled my watch and handed it to him.

"What is this?"

"A clock...A timepiece."

He turned it over and looked at the back and glanced up at me before continuing to study it. The fact that it was solid gold was unmistakable. He squinted at the tiny writing on the back. "Beautiful fine work...but I do not understand." *It was hard for him to admit that.*

"There are two small springs inside that, with the help of gears cause the hands to turn to indicate what the time of day it is."

"Hands?"

"Under the glass are three pointers with arrowheads on the ends. They are all constantly in motion, but too slow to see with the eye, except for the second hand, which turns one revolution per minute. We have divided the time in a day from midnight to midnight into twenty four hours, and each hour into sixty minutes, and each minute into sixty seconds. The shortest of the pointers point towards the hour, the longer one towards the minute, and the moving hand ticks out the seconds."

He could read the Roman numerals on the dial. "The shortest pointer is directed towards the eleven," he said. "And I see no movement."

"What? May I see it?"

Non-plussed, he handed it back. The watch had stopped running, and the time read 10:54. I tried winding it. "Perhaps it's broken." I said—perplexed.

He was stunned. I strode over to the window and looked out. There was no glass in it, just a Romanesque arched opening. "You know, France looks no different now than it does in my day. The birds sing the same songs. They say that it is men who carve and forge history. At times I have wondered: if we were no longer here, would the bird-song change?"

I turned towards him. "I want to continue my initiation through the Serpent Rouge, find my daughter and return to my own time. Otherwise you are stuck with me."

It was a poor joke, but he almost smiled anyway. He stepped over to a side table. "Wine?"

"Yes, thank you."

He reached for a silver flagon and two silver goblets, poured the wine and gestured for me to sit down in a sturdy chair. The wine was deep, red, heady stuff. The Poor Knights of Christ had their pleasures. I did not complain. We drank in silence for awhile.

He was still fingering the one franc coin. "What is its value?"

"One loaf of bread."

"Who is the King of France in your time?"

"There are no longer Monarchs in France."

"How is the country governed then?"

"It's a democracy. The people decide by vote who the temporary rulers and administrators will be. All adults, including women have the right to vote for their representatives."

He was dubious. "Does that system function?"

"In its own way, yes. It can take a long time for decisions to be made, and it has spawned a redundant bureaucracy. But in essence the system honors the sovereignty of the individual." *I thought of communism—that thorn in the side of 20th century political freedom.*

He was interested, so I continued, "There are still a few strict monarchies, but there are also some countries that are governed by a blend of democracy and a monarchy. They are called 'constitutional monarchies'. In that system, the king or queen has no administrative power—like the ability to wage war. Those decisions are made by the governing body. The duty of the monarch is to ensure that the governing body does not begin to seize too much power and take advantage of the common people. The king or queen's job is to protect the people *from* the government."

"That is similar to the way the Merovingian kings governed, and yet they were warriors, and retained the power to wage war."

"Interesting. I know very little concerning the Merovingian dynasty. Much of it was purposefully eliminated from our history books."

His eyes narrowed. "Need I ask who was responsible for that?"

"I was determined not to discuss religion with you, due to the...nature of the Templar order."

"Well...define religion." It was not a question.

"Touché commander." I set my flagon down.

He leaned back in his chair. "If you do end up remaining with us, I would enjoy further discussions. Now I must prepare to entertain some—shall we say—less than savory guests that are traveling from the siege and the *pyre*. It is part of my duties. I will give you a room. Stay in it. You will be shown to the entrance of the labyrinth in the morning." He was still cradling the one Franc coin in his left hand. "May I keep this—in lieu of your entrance fee?"

"Of course." I smiled.

He pushed the old Templar coin back towards me.

"I may need a loaf of bread some *time*."

Shortly after being escorted to a room, a servant brought me a meal—middle ages style: bread, cheese, olives, wine, and a chunk of mutton. It was actually quite good, and there was enough wine to make me drowsy. The bed was a simple wooden palette with straw on it. There were lice in the straw, so I curled up in the opposite corner on the floor; I was so tired I didn't care.

Sometime in the middle of the night I awoke in the dark. I remembered where I was, but didn't want to believe it, hoping I would just wake up out of the dream. It was a hard reality though, like the floor I'd been sleeping on. My right shoulder was sore from pressing into it. The moon was in a pale cycle, but what little of it there was, along with the starlight, framed the single arched window opening with light. I stood up and looked out. There was nothing to see in the dark courtyard below, just the sounds of the horses shuffling and a night bird crying out in the distance. I leaned against the deep stone window sill and breathed in the cool night air. Cooking aromas still wafted up from the kitchen below, mixed with the smell of the horses, along with the taint of human filth. These peoples noses were probably immune to it, but growing up in a more modern era featuring indoor plumbing, I found the ever-present stench here repulsive.

I would not be staying in the middle ages. I would find that time portal and return to my own era. However, the potential for me to go through it to yet another time was a disturbing potential. Why should I assume that the doorway would automatically send me back to my own time—and place? One could only hope that perhaps there was a grander design, a subtle directive not yet discernible in this real-world stage play I had been thrust into. Is there a marionette master, or is it perhaps some underlying part of ourselves that pulls those invisible strings?

Those are some of the things I contemplated while leaning on that rough stone window sill. Presently it was bird time—their time to wake up, but I became drowsy, and slept in a half-awake dream state until I was roused by a knock on the door.

It was my time to enter the labyrinth. The same sergeant that had let me into the keep the day before escorted me out the postern gate, and through the damp foggy morning until we came to a cleverly concealed riveted iron door.

He selected an elaborately designed key on his key ring and unlocked a large, round padlock with crude rivets holding it together. The door squeaked as it swung outwards. As he held it open, he looked at me. He had not spoken a word since he had woken me up. He was not unfriendly, he was just doing his job, but the look said: *you chose to go in there.*

I couldn't vacillate. My male pride would not allow it, especially since it was he who I had petitioned so boldly to allow me into the keep the previous morning.

The door swung shut behind me with a clank, and the padlock snap closed. The only light that entered the room was what bits sneaked in around the door frame. I was still not fully awake, and had a hangover from the heavy wine the night before. I fumbled in my pocket for the Riviera Can-Can matches. One match was enough to orient myself. I was in a kind of anteroom, with rough steps that spiraled downwards to the right. Oddly enough, the steps appeared rounded, as if they had been well trafficked; or used for a very long time. Another match enabled me to determine that there was no candle, torch, or lamp available in the room.

I proceeded in the dark. There were twelve steps down that ended on a platform, which led to a hallway that became rougher the further it progressed. Eventually it was nothing more than a mine shaft that sloped slightly downward. I kept my left hand above my head, and my right hand out in front of me to find my way. The hallway ceiling gradually became lower until I was forced to crawl through it, and eventually shrunk even tighter until I was no longer on my hands and knees.

Out of curiosity, I lit another match. I was indeed crawling through the native rock. Before the light was extinguished I observed the same phenomenon I had noticed on the stairs; the leading edges of the stone passageway were slightly rounded and grimy. How many initiates had crawled through here to polish the stone like that? I came to the conclusion that the passageway must lead somewhere, or there would be corpses in here. Perhaps there were piles of them up ahead somewhere. It was not an inspiring thought. In fact, that is when the seeds of despair were sown.

The passageway became tighter. I tied the wooden document tube to an ankle and drug it behind me. The pistol in my jacket pocket was downright uncomfortable; pressing against my leg and groin. Every time I thought about the potential of running into a corpse my mood darkened. Eventually I became angry; more angry than I had ever been. Swearing, I flailed against the sides of the walls. The cold stone was impassive and unyielding, which elicited even more aggressive action. I pushed forward at a furious pace through the ever tightening passageway until I couldn't move forward—or breath.

That was when the panic came upon me. It wasn't merely claustrophobia; it was far worse than that. It was a *buried alive* fear that reared its ugly head from somewhere deep in my soul—from another lifetime perhaps. From whence it came I do not know and do not care to know. What I went through down in the womb of the earth that morning is difficult to relate. The panic immobilized me. I couldn't back out. I kept trying to force myself to relax, but then another wave of fear would hit me. I hyperventilated until I was totally emotionally exhausted. This could not be the right path. This path led only to darkness, despair, and death. Behind though, was the iron door of humanity; stubbornly ignorant—suspicious of anyone who takes steps to emerge from the quagmire—all the while privately struggling with their own personal demons.

They say time is a healer. I must have laid there for an hour. The waves of fear became less frequent, and I began to take them less seriously.

I thought about Monique, her feet splashing in the shallow river water in the gentle sunshine. I could almost hear the river. I *could* hear the river. Laying there quietly, without moving, I could barely discern the sound of running water coming from up ahead—not far.

With my body relaxed, I began to inch forward like a worm; and like a worm I squirmed ungracefully from my wormhole onto the edge of a wet, rocky underground stream. Painfully, with my hand above my head I stood up. I couldn't feel a ceiling. My body felt like it was bruised all over, and had lost its equilibrium. I reached out to steady myself on the wall above the wormhole.

I had only been about twenty feet from the opening when I had panicked. I stood there and thought about that for awhile. It was important. How fickle we are. How much of our suffering is unnecessary and self-inflicted? How much of our time do we spend self-promoting our own personal discontent?

Monsieur Lecuyer had told me I may need to cross an underground river, so I turned and stepped into it, not feeling particularly good about myself. The stones were slippery, and as the river became deeper the more self-respect I lost. Self-respect? Why do I waste my time endeavoring to make myself feel good *about* myself? Because I am actually weak and selfish. Everything I do is motivated by self gratification. I am lying to myself if I think otherwise. The cowardly lie varnishes over my pathetic fears, but the thin varnish never really dries, having been applied in a cold, damp room in the recesses of my soul. It remains foul-smelling and sticky. I hope no one can smell it, but they do anyway. It's stuck to my hands and body. I fear it might incur pain if I try to wash it off. I make a lame attempt to keep the door of the room closed, but it's frame is crumbled and rotting.

What about the important things I believe in? Human love?—What a farce. Paratge?—A fantasy for the poetic. Kindness?—Just another feel-good shot in the arm. How about my purported love for humanity? Is that not a noble, admirable aspiration? No—it's all meaningless. I am faux—a fake. That's why those smelly gargoyles sneer and laugh at me. *They know.*

There was nothing left of me. All of my hopes, aspirations—everything I had lived for and believed in had been stripped away. All that remained was a hollow vacuum of despair. The water was cold and cruel, and became so deep that I thought I may have to swim. It was flowing almost too swiftly for me to walk through. I would be swept downstream and deposited in the log-jam with the rest of the corpses: the flotsam and jetsam of humanity. My legs moved in slow motion through the water—one step at a time.

The river began to become shallower. I realized that the underground stream was like a part of my subconscious, flowing steadily with its own agenda, sometimes running contrary to the more obvious stream on the surface. My daily life was like a small sailboat, struggling in the wind to tack back and forth. I tried to keep the little boat on course, but at times it would be blown off in a storm or found dallying on the surface. Unseen under the water a powerful submarine glided silently, sliding through the depths. Occasionally the craft would surface, but usually it traveled just under the rippling, undulating waves. At times I could see it, as I peered over the gunnel into the depths. The powerful ship was infinitely patient, and would pause and wait for me at times, when I flitted frivolously above.

By the time I had made the crossing and stood dripping on the shore I had come to realize that there was, in fact something left of me; that facet that is always in the background with endless patience, urging, goading, inspiring. It is the artist's muse, where my truth pictures come from—my elven self. It is the eternal part of me that is capable of doing anything.

That was all that remained. The river had cleansed me of my demons.

I lit a match.

There were several openings—different paths one could choose. I was standing directly in front of the one I knew to be my path. How I knew I cannot describe. I dropped the match and moved into the opening in the void left by the extinguished light. The way went uphill. It was not a struggle.

I thought about the potential of seeing in the dark. Colors began to flash in my field of vision. It was as if my brain had received a directive and was beginning to work out the logistics. Reveling in the colors my mind began to imagine many things—to roam free. Invisible boundaries had somehow been removed. It felt like any thought that I entertained would begin a process, turning wheels into motion so that anything that I imagined could occur.

Presently I came to broad, straight stairway. As I began to climb I noticed a distinct high frequency ringing in my ears, which increased as I continued upwards. At times I had heard that ringing near the sacred spring, but this was more intense. Olivier had said that the Paris Meridian and the old Rose Line came right through the area. I ascended a long stairway with over thirty steps until I felt a smooth, flat floor under my feet. A dim light shone from far ahead. When I began to move toward the light I noticed that my wet leather-soled shoes were conjuring up completely different sounds—flat multiple echoes.

I was in a vast, underground room. As I approached the light, I realized that I was walking between large, ornate columns spaced about twenty feet apart.

The natural light filtered down from an opening in the ceiling high above. Beyond lay four pedestals, and an altar. On the altar was a candle in a large candle holder. I lit it, feeling like I was a player in a play acting out a prearranged part. The altar was decorated with a menagerie of symbols—some I recognized, like the fleur-de-lis and the Maltese cross, but there was also what appeared to be Arabic as well as Latin inscriptions on the walls. The pedestals were arranged in a semi-circle in front of the altar. On one pedestal sat a stone lion with a paw up and claws out, on another perched a dragon. A unicorn stood on a third, and a bear on the fourth—all guardians facing outwards.

I picked up the candle holder to investigate further. It was heavy—solid gold. I moved to the column to the left of the altar. It was very ornate, with grapevines in an organic pattern spiraling up to multiple symbols above. Beyond the column sat a tomb, with inscriptions in Latin on it. Near the tomb was an arched grotto with artifacts and a wooden box resting on a single shelf. The candle produced enough light for me to see that there were more objects and artifacts deeper in the underground temple. I had no interest in disturbing any of that, so I investigated the area to the right side of the altar. There was nothing there except a doorway. In contrast to the ornate decorations nearby the doorway was just a simple cased opening, with only one symbol carved into the keystone in the arch--a five pointed star with the point up. That was my pathway.

I returned to the altar, set the candle holder back in its place and blew out the candle, where it could wait for the next initiate to use it. I stood there for awhile with my eyes closed, aware of the persistent ringing in my ears. I decided that the rest of my life would be devoted to the Great Work, which for me meant exploring and perfecting my abilities, and encouraging the same in others. If I strayed I would not be hard on myself as I had been in the past. I would just continue on the path, one step at a time.

I opened my eyes, looked at the altar area one last time, and strode through the doorway under the initiate's star, up the corridor and out into the sunlight.

It was so bright that I had to shield my eyes. The sun was hot, causing steam to begin to rise from my damp trousers. This time, I could see the trail. It was greener, just as Monique had claimed. Exhilarated, I moved down it, and came to a pool lined with stones in the middle of a triangular field. It was fed by a spring and had a large stone on one end. I washed my face and hands in it—once again feeling like an actor in a play. Not far from the pool I saw what looked like the portal.

It was greener even than the trail and there was movement around it—creatures. Monique was always talking about them, but I had never seen them before. They hid when I approached. There was only one thing to do. I put in my mind where I wanted to go and stepped through the portal.

There was a shift, and the light changed. I could see where I was. The stone chair was in the distance. The portal had moved further away from it. I was so excited that I ran towards the chair. Monique was there placing stones in a circle in the river shallows. She looked up as I picked her up and hugged her. She smelled musky and flowery. I didn't want to let go. The little girl wiggled out of my arms.

"Papa, you were gone so long!" Monique was worried and upset. She looked at my face. "You're bleeding, and you need to shave." I was speechless. "Mama won't wake up. I tried to wake her."

Céline was lying asleep under the tree as she had been when I left. She was breathing normally with the handkerchief over her eyes.

Kneeling next to her, I lightly put my hand on her stomach. "Céline?" There was no response, so I tried harder. "Céline, my lovely...my fairy queen...Arise!.. It's Oberon...Wake up!"

"Why don't you just kiss her and wake her up Papa?" Monique chirped. Sleeping Beauty was her favorite story. I had read it to her over and over at bedtimes. Turning towards Monique, I saw that the girl was totally serious. Why not? It was worth a try, so I gave Céline a little soft kiss on her lips. When nothing happened I felt foolish and sat back on my heels. Monique pouted.

Céline opened her eyes. It was amazing.

Delighted, Monique shrieked, clapped her hands and began dancing around in circles like a pixie. "Papa is prince charming!...Papa is prince charming!"

It was a moment I will never, ever, ever forget.

I bathed in the sight of my wife.

She reached up and touched my face. "What happened to you? You need to shave."

I laughed, "Yes...that is what Monique said."

Realization came into her face, "You did it didn't you?"

I nodded my head in a little yes.

Timidly, she touched my forearm. "I am sorry that we quarreled. I shouldn't have gotten angry."

It seemed like an eternity ago, and bore little weight for me now. I had changed.

There was only one scene left for the actor—one more preordained task to perform. I sat in the huge stone chair and bathed my feet in the water that bubbled out of the ground next to it.

After I cleaned up in a hotel room, I put my extra set of cloths on only to realize that my watch was running perfectly and exactly on time—in 1949.

That evening, we had dinner outside at a little restaurant. I took everything in—en-joyed it all, and ordered much of what was on the menu. My two ladies, tall and small, didn't know quite what to make of me. We had far too much food on the table. I was typically frugal by habit, and would finish everything on my plate. Earlier I had seen an old lady in worn clothes enter her home on the other side of the square. She was alone. I took a big plate of food over and knocked on the door.

Normally I would never be so bold.

"Excuse me Madame, but we ordered too much food and my daughter is not particularly hungry (I fibbed). Would you mind? You can return the plate to the restaurant later."

For a moment I thought she was going to refuse, but she took the plate, mumbled a "Merci", started to close the door, but stopped, looked up and held my gaze. "Congratulations Monsieur." She was serious, and shut the door.

The locals are steeped in the legends and privy to what goes on in their environment.

It was something to keep in mind when in France. Even after living there for several years, I still had difficulty grasping the relationship between the blatantly pagan local folklore and the strictly religious dogma. That they were in bed together was certain, but what went on behind closed doors remained a mystery— much like my wife. Even after being married and close with her for several years, she remained an enigma. I still had no idea what went on inside that gorgeous head much of the time. With Céline, one expects her to harbor secrets. She is a walking secret. I tend to be more of an open book. One would think that Céline knows everything about me. Perhaps that is why she became so upset when my dirty little pot-o-gold secret surfaced. For her, my open nature had been a stabilizing factor in a foggy, clandestine world. To discover that the open book actually had his own secrets had fractured some of that fragile notion of stability.

21

Return From Le Serpent Rouge

Monsieur Lecuyer questioned Monique first. "So...Mademoiselle Monique, I heard you went on a little adventure in Le Serpent Rouge!"

"It was a big adventure. I met a beautiful princess who looked just like mama, but she was younger. She gave me Rupert." Monique said.

"Rupert?"

She held out the jade elephant. He examined it closely. "This should be in a museum," he mumbled.

"He doesn't like museums. They are stuffy and boring." Monique replied defensively. "He likes jungles." She stepped up and took it out of his hand. It was almost rude. Monique could be quite bold.

He stifled a laugh.

"Of course, I should have known that." He continued. "Did the princess tell you her name?"

"Princess Aliénor."

He looked incredulous. "You met a princess that

looked much like your mother and went by the name of Aliénor?"

"Yes, when I first saw her, I thought she was Mama. She was surrounded by a bunch of ladies, and trying on her wedding dress."

"Did she—by chance happen to mention who she was going to marry?"

"Prince Louis Ca...Ca."

"Prince Louis Capet?"

"Yes, but I don't think she was very happy about it." Monique said seriously.

Monsieur Lecuyer paused, stared, and then exploded with a laugh so loud that it frightened Monique. He put a hand over his mouth and then gestured outwards with it. "Monique, you have been fortunate enough to meet one of the most famous women in all of European history. We know of her as Eleanor d'Aquitane. Shortly after you met her, she became Queen of France, and later was Queen of England for many years. She was the mother of many children, including Richard Coeur de Lion, and the infamous prince John. Today there are some that would cut off an appendage to have the honor just to meet her."

At that, Monique made a face. "She was nice to me. She let me sleep on her bed."

"That's good to know," he said. "There are some today that are of the opinion that she was a wanton dragon lady."

"No, she was sweet. Her lady-in-waiting was the dragon lady."

"Really!"

Monique was incurably charming, and continued

234

telling the rest of her story in detail. Céline and I had heard some of it already.

When it came time for me to relate my story I demurred. It was so personal I wasn't sure whether I wanted to even talk about it. Monsieur Lecuyer urged me to pass it on to the Priory, at least for the sake of history. He told me that in his memory, no one had even come close to doing what Monique, Céline and I had done in Le Serpent Rouge.

Olivier and Céline listened as I related the experience in as much detail as I could recall. He asked a few questions, and took some notes. I finished the story with me washing my feet in the "devils armchair". Apparently that was what they called it.

"Well," he said. "May I see the document?"

"Oh, I'm sorry, I almost forgot." The document tube had been leaning up against the divan next to me. I handed him the whole thing. It was heavily scratched, and a crack ran the length of it. He took it over to a table, carefully removed the cap, and gently extracted the rolled-up parchment from it. Switching on a desk lamp, he studied it for awhile.

"Have you read this?" He said.

"No, I doubt that I could. I haven't even looked at it."

He stepped over and handed it to me. "Is it, by chance familiar to you?"

It was, but at first I couldn't place it. Then I realized where I had seen it before. It had the bishop's rose stamp on the top, his signature on the bottom—and my name on it!

"This is the document I put in the wall in 1944 at the l'ermitage ancienne!"

235

"No Marc...That was a copy...*This* is the original!"

I was shocked. "How can that be?" I blurted out. "What are the chances I could end up with the very same document?"

"Do you really believe in chances?"

"Well...mathematically..."

"Forget mathematics," he cut in. "Let me ask you this. How did you feel when you and Jacques failed to retrieve the copy from l'ermitage ancienne?"

"How did I feel? I was humiliated. I, who am interested in archeology and a history buff, had my hands on a rare, valuable document and I forgot about it, blundering like a total idiot. I am still embarrassed about it!" I paused. "It didn't help to have Jacques passing judgment on me."

Olivier flipped his hand backwards. "Don't mind Jacques. He sneers at everyone."

I thought about the gargoyles. "I know, but I humiliated myself."

"There are times when we are our own worst enemies, are we not?" He said quietly, raising his eyebrows before continuing his query. "When you and Jacques realized that the document had disappeared, how determined were you to get it back?"

"Very much so." I wasn't sure if I wanted to admit the depth of it. Céline had been listening, and was looking at the document, and Monique was in the far corner playing with the elephant. I knew better—children hear all.

It was time for a buffered truth. "At that moment in time sir, with my pistol in my pocket I would be considered, shall we say...rather dangerous." I admitted quietly. Céline looked up.

Olivier was not to be sidetracked, and continued with his thread. "So you wanted passionately to get the document back--therefore you did didn't you?"

"I didn't plan it that way!"

"Are you sure? The first person you visited was the very man you needed to draft it!"

I was stubborn. "I certainly did not intend on going to the middle ages. It stank there!"

He laughed. "My dear boy. There are many different parts of our beings that operate in many levels simultaneously. We function on multiple levels of consciousness. When a person is very passionate about something, it is like an automatic signal that's given to a higher, more powerful part of them. Reality then begins to bend and move in that direction."

I thought about how I felt after crossing the underground river beneath the temple. At that point I knew I could do anything with my mind.

Monsieur Lecuyer pressed no further. It was a delicate moment. He settled himself into his comfortable chair. "Cognac?" He offered.

"Yes sir, thank you." I said respectfully.

Céline, Olivier, and I sipped the Cognac quietly as we entertained our own thoughts.

Later, I felt that I needed to address a key question that had been bothering me. "I still don't understand what is so important about a specific genetic bloodline? Okay, so there is an ancestral connection to Jesus. So what? That was a long time ago. With all due respects sir, it has the flavor of a 'holier than thou' attitude."

"Your friend Raoul's assessment." He chided.

"I didn't mean it that way."

"But I like it. How did he put it? 'Obsessed with the notion of being old French royalty'."

I chided him back. "You really like the 'obsessed' part don't you?"

"Well, it makes one feel like a rabid dog. One small stumble further towards insanity and one would become 'possessed'."

"I don't think you're quite there yet sir."

"I'm glad I have your support, Marc." He looked out the window for a moment. "Did you, by chance read the copy of The Epic of Gilgamesh I gave you?"

"Yes. A rather odd collection of stories."

"How so?" He asked.

"Well...Gilgamesh seems so childlike and arrogant. As a prince he was probably a spoiled brat. He runs around the countryside stirring up trouble with his ape-like friend."

Olivier laughed. "In all of my studies of Sumerology, this is first time I have heard Gilgamesh referred to as a 'spoiled brat'."

"I wondered if at the time of his adventures he was king of the city-state or still a prince? The translation suggested that he was king. As a prince he would have been freer to sow his wild oats, but as a king one would think he would have more pressing responsibilities."

"Good point, and one we do not have the answer to. Others may argue differently though. Translations are always in question. Those tales have been pieced together using fragments from Sumerian, Akkadian and Assyrian sources. All of those cultures, including the Babylonians and Hebrews used the same creation stories. Did you recognize the similarity between one of the stories and a famous biblical tale?"

"Sure. Wasn't that one guy Noah? What was his name?"

"Ziusudra. Not a common American name."

"No. If I have a son I will probably not choose to name him that. But that story was different than the version from the bible."

"It's the original version, and much more complete. It predated the Hebrew rendition by over 2300 years. What was your impression of it?"

"It is interesting that he traveled so far to find what? He went through what sounded like an underground area or cave for days before reaching 'the garden of the gods', which seemed like a vast region. Before finding Noah, he encountered the lady that made wine—Siduri, with her 'golden bowl and golden vat'. He was a prince or a king, and she talked down to him. If she was a goddess, she seemed fairly flesh and blood to me!"

"Good questions, and one of my favorite parts. May I?" He got up and pulled a copy out of a bookshelf, sat back down and flipped through the pages.

"Ah, here it is...Remember: Gilgamesh—rough, unkempt, an arrogant, tries to push through the gate into her vineyard. Siduri apprehends him and it angers her. She then speaks very directly to him."

Why is despair in your heart and your face like the face of one who has made a long journey? Yes, why is your face burned from the heat and the cold, and why do you come here wandering in search of the wind?

"After he tells her of his quest, she offers him some practical advice:"

> As for you Gilgamesh, fill your belly with good things; day and night, night and day, dance and be merry, feast and rejoice. Let your clothes be fresh, bath yourself in water, cherish the little child that holds your hand, and make your wife happy in your embrace; for this too is the lot of man.

"Good advice, no?" He asked.

"Yes, but what makes Gilgamesh a hero is that he challenges what most consider to be normal."

"Yes! And that is what we are leading to. What was he challenging? What was Gilgamesh seeking?"

I thought about it. "I am not sure."

"That is your assignment. I will not acquiesce to answer the question for you, but I will give you a clue: Who was Gilgamesh's mother?"

He handed me the copy he had been reading from and two more books from the shelf. They were hardcore Sumerology—in French.

My French language reading skills were at perhaps the sixth grade level, causing me to struggle with the scholarly text in the books. Céline helped me with some of the difficult parts, and after two days I felt that I understood. At the breakfast table I related my ideas to Olivier and Céline. Monique listened as well.

"Gilgamesh's father was a human, but his mother was what they called an Anunnaki—one of their goddesses.

She lived in the palace in the city, attended by ladies in waiting. The Anunnaki had a numerical rating system based on their genealogy which defined how important an individual was in their hierarchy. His mother was lower on the totem pole, but was nevertheless one of them. Apparently, the Anunnaki could die, but normally lived very long life spans; what humans may consider immortal. Since Gilgamesh's father was human, and his mother was an Anunnaki, he didn't know how long he would live for. So my conclusion is that Gilgamesh was essentially seeking his own immortality."

Olivier produced his Mona Lisa smile once again.

I continued. "Many of the old tales from indigenous peoples and other ancient cultures seem to be symbolical or allegorical for the most part. 'Father Sky and Mother Earth' etc.. Many were probably dreamed up around the campfire at some point to teach social behavior."

"The Sumerian tales don't have that flavor. There is little instruction on social behavior and scant symbology. One could try to attach allegory to them, but you can do that to anything. Frankly, their tales are graphic and disturbing."

I was on a roll. "That got me to thinking about Ziusudra. Here he was living by himself in some far-off corner of the 'garden of the gods' in retirement. When he told Gilgamesh the tale of the Deluge, it seemed like the event he was describing had happened long before that—like thousands of years before. How old was he? Was he one of the Anunnaki? In the Old Testament genealogy, Noah is one of the key ancestors of the Semitic peoples, a progeny of Eve herself. According to the Bible, those patriarchs lived incredibly long life spans, but as generations passed their lifespans decreased in a linear fashion. Gilgamesh reigned for 120 years."

"Who were the Anunnaki really? They seemed to possess superior technology, but not the kind of advanced spirituality or occult powers like we associate with angels or gods. They regularly fought amongst themselves, like the Greek gods but even more ruthlessly. I hesitate to draw conclusions but they seem more like people than 'gods' to me. Were the Sumerian people really so stupid and delusional as to resort to making up a completely fictitious set of gods and goddesses that they imagined lived amongst them?"

Monsieur Lecuyer raised his eyebrows. "That is what our historians would like us to believe. Even a scientifically minded person will inevitably select or interpret data through the filter of their own personal belief systems. It is our Achilles heel, so to speak."

What actually transpired afterwards is interesting. Monique's story became, by far the most famous inside the Priory, due to the fact that she had met a historical celebrity and because she was a child. My experience, even though it was—for me much more profound, fifty years later became sloughed off into scholarly obscurity. In fact, there were some within the Priory that didn't believe it was true, claiming I had fabricated it in an effort to gloss over my ineptitude in disregarding the parchment document as unimportant. *The snobs were envious.*

When I related my story to Olivier, he took notes. Later he told me that from the historical records he had access to, Betrand Marty was in fact the head of the

Cathar Perfecti and the Bishop of Toulouse, but possibly in name only, as he had served in the position in Toulouse for a brief time, if at all. Rixende de Telle appears in history with few references, but she was affirmed as the head of the female Perfectae—the equivalent of a mother superior in the Roman Catholic church. Both were burned along with two hundred other Cathars following the surrender of Montségur.

The Templar commander, Raymond de Bures is unknown, and has slipped through the cracks of history. For me Raymond was a live, vital, powerful, influential character. It led me to thinking. How many people in history are completely overlooked or have been forgotten? We remember a scant few celebrities, conquerors, and famous artists. Perhaps the "golden thread that weaves through time" are those who have carried the torch bravely, but without historical recognition. Does that mean their contributions carried no weight? There are some, like the Prieuré de Sion, that purposefully work behind the scenes. The Sufi order is another good example, and has continuously influenced eastern and western thought with scant organization and no interest in domination.

We remember the Caesars, the Alexanders, and the Cleopatras—who would all probably be diagnosed as narcissistic megalomaniacs by modern psychiatrists.

The similarities between Monique's experience and my own are obvious, the most curious being the fact that both of us met women that bore a striking resemblance to Céline. That remains a mystery that I ponder to this day.

22

D.C. al Coda

Many years later, in 1972, most of the players in this story were gone. Monique had her own life, and Celine and I were living comfortably. Young people were on the move, and it seemed as if the world was indeed changing.

After taking care of some business in Geneva, I came to the fork in the road. Many times I had thought of returning there, but it had never felt right or I was somehow too busy. This time, like Le Serpent Rouge, the road to the right was greener—beckoning me. Without thinking, I went that way. It felt good once again to do something on impulse. It was late summer—the same time of year when I first had visited the place. The road had been repaired and paved. It didn't take long to get there. It was as if the entire environs had shrunk in size.

The track to the l'ermitage ancienne was overgrown with foliage, but I forced my expensive auto through it. I didn't care.

A wisp of gray smoke curled out of the chimney. As I got out of the car a frightened young man appeared in the doorway.

"I am sorry sir, we just needed a place to sleep for the night."

He looked like a young Adonis, or a prince of the Mérovée with his long hair and bronzed skin.

I held my hand up. "It's alright. How did you find it?"

He stammered. "We were hitchhiking, and walking up the hill towards the mountains. We saw the track and thought it was perhaps a place we could camp for the night. The door of the cottage was open so..."

I interrupted him. "I hope that the door of this cottage always remains open. Why don't you stay another day?"

A part of him understands.

A lovely young lady came out. *He is protecting her.* They were both very young and attractive. I rarely see auras, but I caught the hint of a single yellow glow surrounding both of them. The young lovers looked like brother and sister. *They had been drinking the water.*

"Actually, I don't want to disturb you, but I would like to go down the trail behind the l'ermitage and visit a place I know of."

"Trail?" The Adonis asked.

"May I show you?"

They followed me around the building, and I pointed down over the cliff. "If you do choose to stay, I recommend that you visit the sacred spring below."

"Sacred spring?" The young lady asked.

"You'll know it when you find it. There is a dolmen there."

"A dolmen!" She exclaimed, as if it were a thing of grandiose magical proportions.

Without further adieu, I stepped over the rock and began to pick my way down the goat path. I looked up to see their tanned beautiful faces watching me.

The sacred spring was exactly as I had remembered. A hawk soared far over head, the current sentinel. I stayed there for awhile. There were no revelations, no visitations or mystical experiences. It was simply peaceful and quiet, with the backdrop of the intoxicating sound of the water as it fell into the pool. I drank some of it out of the stone cup and placed the artifact back at the foot of the standing stone. I found myself staring at the cup.

The stone cup, as unassuming as it is—is the oldest artifact here. It once used to reside in the secret cave upstream.

When I had finally made my way back up the trail and stepped over the rock the young lovers were sitting on the stone bench. I had to stop and catch my breath before I filled my water bottle out of the swirling pool.

"Do you know who made the whirlpool sir?" The young lady asked.

I shook my head. "That's long before my time."

"I saw little flashes of light by the pool!" She was excitable.

"My daughter used to watch the fairies as they danced around this pool." I waited to see how they would react. I felt no judgment.

The young man spoke up. "You called this place a l'ermitage?"

"It has been called the l'ermitage ancienne, and has been a refuge for those who can find it." I looked at the young man, and then over at the lady. "And for those

247

who can see the little lights by the pool." I produced my own version of the Mona Lisa smile, nodded, and took my leave.

When I opened the door to my car, I remembered the two cases of Hermitage that I had picked up earlier in Valence. *Perfect.* On impulse, I snatched one of the bottles out of the case, quietly opened the front door to the l'ermitage, and set the bottle on the table amongst their camping gear.

I stopped in front of the chateau and stepped outside of the car. A shade tree sheltered the stairs going into the cellar, and tall, almost spent bright flowers leaned over in front of the stonework of the house. A small vegetable garden tenaciously clung to the cliff face.

"Can I help you?" A women appeared with garden gloves on.

"My apologies for the intrusion, but I was just stopping to...admire the beauty of your home."

"Tourists will stop and snap photos, but they usually stay in their cars."

"Once again, I am sorry for bothering you." I saw a little boy running behind the house.

She studied me for a moment. "They say that it was built by an eccentric American."

I shook my head. "You know how those crazy Americans can be!"

She had heard my accent. "It was you wasn't it?"

I hedged. "Why do you think that?"

"Sometimes I just know things."

I nodded my head in appreciation. "Then this is a good place for you to be."

She had heard the stories.

"Would you like to come in for a cup of tea?"

"No, but thank you for the kind offer. This is your home now. Is Father Bouchet still here?"

"Why yes, of course."

"I will pay him a little visit then."

I bid her good day and went into the village. The street was lined with trees, and wooden boxes brimming with scarlet and indigo flowers. There was a new bakery and small general store. The little hamlet had made the transition from quaint to charming.

My timing was auspicious. Robert was at home, and just settling in for the evening with a glass of wine.

We drank a bottle of the Altesse from Xavier's vineyards and reminisced. We didn't bother to mention the Priory, murder, the church, or politics. We talked about the town with its new additions. A new housing development had sprouted up in one of the old cow pastures below, which would fill up in the winter with skiers. It was annoying, and upsetting to the placid routine of the village, but had brought some refreshing revenue in. As a proud parent, I told him about Monique, and her new life as an adult.

When I stepped out onto the street I turned to bid him farewell. As he stood in the doorway, the golden light from the setting sun illuminated his hazel eyes.

He confessed. "You know I have been looking after the sacred spring."

"I noticed how tidy it is. So you are the caretaker now?"

He nodded with a satisfied kind of pride.

I raised my eyebrows. "Perhaps there is hope after all."

The Sacred Spring of the Blood Royal
The Secret Order of the Grail

Mark Stanley

Formatted using InDesign CS5.
Typeset in 12 point Adobe Garamond Pro.
The display face is also Adobe Garamond Pro.
The title faces are Charlemagne, and Trajan Pro.
Numbering in Trajan Pro.

Cover design by Alexandra Shostak
coversbyalexandra@gmail.com

Printed in the United States of America.

Made in the USA
San Bernardino, CA
01 February 2013